Fidelio

Fidelio

My Voyage to a Distant Shore

Rodger Bridwell

TT TRUMAN TALLEY BOOKS / E. P. DUTTON / NEW YORK

Published in the United States by
Truman Talley Books • E. P. Dutton,
a division of New American Library,
2 Park Avenue, New York, N.Y. 10016.

Library of Congress Cataloging-in-Publication Data

Bridwell, Rodger.
Fidelio: my voyage to a distant shore.
"Truman Talley books."
1. Bridwell, Rodger.   2. Fidelio (Boat)
3. Voyages and travels—1951–   .   I. Title.
G470.B79B75   1986   910.4'5   86-2091

ISBN: 0-525-24397-6

Published simultaneously in Canada by
Fitzhenry & Whiteside Limited, Toronto

W

DESIGNED BY MARK O'CONNOR

10   9   8   7   6   5   4   3   2   1

First Edition

FOR KATHERINE—

who suffered more waiting than I did sailing

The sea never changes and its works,
for all the talk of men,
are wrapped in mystery.

—JOSEPH CONRAD,
Typhoon

Contents

Contents

Fidelio

Prologue

I am helpless. Completely at the mercy of the implacable sea. Fidelio *slides down the face of these two- and three-story waves like an elevator, leaving the same weightless feeling in my stomach. At the bottom of each trough when the toe rail dips under I expect her to roll over and sink. I say to myself: "If I survive this and reach land safely I will never again leave it. What am I doing out here anyway?"**

SEPTEMBER 13TH: I'm worn out. For the past fifteen months I've been working from eight to ten hours a day, six days a week, building *Fidelio*'s cabin, finishing the interior, and then installing the hundred and more fittings that combine to make a sailboat seaworthy. For example, mast, rigging, pulpits, windlass, self-steering gear, to name only a few.

Actually, the Hydrovane self-steering unit arrived

---

*That paragraph was entered in the ship's log during a gale of near-hurricane force off Cape Finisterre when I figured my chances of survival were about one in ten. What *was* I doing out there?

only this morning—at last. I had about given up hope. So I devote this afternoon to sawing off the stainless steel upper pulpit crossbar, which is in the way, and drilling holes at appropriate places in the transom. Then I offer up a devout prayer that it fits and works. I'll bolt it on after dinner and insert the rudder with the aid of the dinghy.

If it all falls into place, tomorrow morning I will bid farewell to the good old Lady Bee Marina and Shoreham-by-the-Sea, head down Channel, destination Antigua, West Indies, where some two hundred years ago Lord Nelson headquartered his fleet between battles with the French.

I drop below, look at the stove, and consider my cooking with distaste. My last night ashore calls for something a little more exotic than chili or spaghetti. In spite of fatigue I change into my shore-going clothes, climb the endless stairs beside the Lady Bee offices, and continue on up the hill to the local pub, which serves surprisingly good food.

I'm early and lucky enough to get a windowside table where I can see the marina, the lock, ship channel, and the English Channel just beyond. A Shell tanker glides out of the lock on its way to the tank farm at Portslade, which is near Brighton.

The prospect of shoving off in the morning should fill me with a sense of fulfillment and joy. And, indeed, I am thankful that the monotonous, exhausting work on the boat is coming to an end. Why, then, am I depressed and apprehensive, not to say plain scared? Perhaps I'm just stale and need a change.

More to the point: What am I doing here all alone?

Why am I here at all? What have I committed myself to?

I think back to the catastrophe—or so it seemed at the time—that indirectly brought me here tonight. When, without any warning, a federal agency issued a complaint against our company on the most flimsy of technicalities. This, nevertheless, forced us out of business.* As a result, we had to refund more than $100,000 to our subscribers. With all the other shutdown expenses our living scale slid downhill like a locomotive out of control.

When the dust cleared we had a little capital left, but nowhere near enough to maintain our luxurious home, with pool service, gardener, and all the rest. In short, a complete break from the past was indicated. As it happened, we had friends living in Spain who were continually urging us to join them because, among other attractions, you could live in style there for about half of what it cost in the States. At that point it didn't take much to convince us, so we sold our home and moved to Spain.

I concentrate on the excellent baked sole and let my mind run back to the second reason for being here. After drifting around Spain for a year, I became increasingly restless. Inevitably, my recurring dream of voyaging under sail surfaced once again. This time instead of sailing across the Pacific, we would cruise the Mediterranean to Istanbul via Sardinia, Malta, the Greek Isles, and Troy. If Hammond Innes could do it, so could we.

I had been looking for a suitable sailboat ever since arriving in Spain. I still hadn't found one when I became

*I was editorial director; my wife, Kathy, was business manager.

convinced that the best material for boat hulls was ferro-cement. I also read about a shipyard in England that was turning out state-of-the-art ferrocement hulls. In a moment of madness I ordered a hull and decided to come to England where I would complete the boat myself.

Meanwhile, it had become all too evident that Kathy and Margaret, our youngest daughter, really didn't want to spend a year aboard a sailboat, not even cruising among the Isles of Greece.

So, I let it be, and decided this would give me an opportunity to test and prove myself by sailing my new boat singlehanded back across the Atlantic. Accordingly, Kathy and Marg returned to the United States, while I headed for England.

While driving across France I decided to name my new boat *Fidelio*—or "faithful one"—after the title of Beethoven's only opera. At Boulogne I caught the ferry to Folkstone, in England, then drove to Maidstone where the freeway begins and so on to the shipyard in Biggin Hill, where the famous World War II airbase is located.

And finally, I'm here due to the magic of a book published forty years ago. When I was a landlocked impressionable teenager I read and reread W. R. Robinson's *Ten Thousand Leagues Over the Sea*. Robinson sailed his 32-footer, *Svaap*, around the world back in the days when stockbrokers were jumping out of hotel windows. Then I could more easily identify with Robinson when he shacked up with an island beauty than I could with the Walter Mittys. So I swore to emulate Robinson, which is probably why, in later life, I became a stockbroker (but not for long).

However, today, unlike Robinson, I am no longer young nor am I an experienced sailor. The latter may account, in part at least, for the sense of impending doom that weighs me down. For I must be the least experienced sailor who ever set out to sail alone across an ocean. Most singlehanders have raced with an Admiral's Cup contender, crewed to Bermuda, or sailed on a Southern Ocean Circuit yacht.

In contrast, I have spent only one night on a sailboat at sea and that was hove to in the fog. All told I have amassed an impressive sailing record! One afternoon sailing *Fidelio,* when I should have had at least a short shakedown cruise before setting out. Back in the States I managed to get in seven days and one night sailing *Goldenrod,* the trimaran I built shortly before moving to Spain. Before that seven daysails with a friend who owned a 32-foot ketch. Until then I had never been on a boat smaller than an auto ferry.

This lack of sailing experience may explain my fears, but will I survive it? Am I on a suicide mission?

When I finish eating I close my eyes and meditate for ten minutes. Then I leave and slowly walk back to the long flight of stairs that descend to the dock where *Fidelio* is moored.

I stand there a while admiring my boat. To me she is a thing of beauty rocking gently beneath the dim marina lights. *Fidelio* is a Hartley 32 ferrocement sloop, designed by a New Zealand naval architect. Twenty-seven feet on the water line, with a 10-foot, 3-inch beam, she's a little on the fat side. Her sister ships raced successfully down under so I hope her English-built hull is as lightweight as those built in New Zealand. If not she will be slower. I shall know very soon.

On board, when I light my pipe and reach for the sherry bottle I feel filled with an inner serenity that has been absent for too long. Is it due to the meditation or the best meal I've had in ages?

No matter, I finish my pipe and go up on deck and actually attack the problem of installing the Hydrovane with feelings of euphoria, determined to embark tomorrow on the voyage that will be an ultimate test of courage. I pray that tomorrow will begin a new and better phase of my life and the lives of those I love.

Midnight—The Hydrovane is in place and it only took two hours! Before going to bed I reread a letter from Valerie, my oldest daughter. I cut out one section where she says:

I BELIEVE IN YOU
I KNOW YOU CAN DO IT

I pin this on the bulkhead beside my statue of a thirteenth-century pilgrim en route to the shrine of St. James, in Santiago de Compostela, Spain.

PART I

*Across the Bay
of Biscay*

Down the
English Channel

Supplication, worship, prayer are not superstition. They are acts more real than the acts of eating, drinking or walking. It is no exaggeration to say that they alone are real, all else is unreal.

—GANDHI

SEPTEMBER 14TH: Departure day! When we (*Fidelio* and RB) motored into Shoreham lock for the last time, we were 225 miles from the Lizard lighthouse, which marks the end of the English Channel and the beginning of the Atlantic Ocean. Even a slow sailboat (which *Fidelio* turned out to be) should be able to negotiate this distance in two or three days. It took us twenty-eight days!

Most of the last day and night are spent fitting the self-steering gear, which had arrived only yesterday from Nottingham, in northern England. The sleepless night seems less important than the good-weather forecast, so I decide to leave this morning. It's a heavenly day, cloudless and windless, as we motor out of Shoreham. At 10:30 A.M. we pass within one hundred feet of the Owers Light Tower and I compare the dead calm with the raging seas of a few days before, when *Morning Cloud* sank. How did the tower survive? It doesn't look that strong.

Early this month, some of the worst gales on record, together with rare waterspouts, roared through the English Channel. At times the wind blew with hurricane force so hard that *Fidelio* was secured with nine mooring lines even though our berth was well protected.

One of the victims of this Force-10 (55 to 63 miles-per-hour winds) storm was the former prime minister's famous Admiral's Cup yacht, *Morning Cloud*. She sank opposite Shoreham, was raised and deposited on the beach only a couple of hundred yards from where *Fidelio* was moored.

I, of course, walked over to look at the sad wreck. She looked as if she had been split down the middle by a meat cleaver. There was a gaping hole in her bottom where the keel and engine had been, while the entire starboard side of hull, deck, and cabin was missing. My guess is that the severe damage resulted from her being pounded on the bottom during the week before she was raised by the two local trawlers whose nets fouled her.

Needless to say, this sight was a bit unnerving. After all, if a 45-foot ocean racer manned by an experienced crew of seven could sink in the English Channel, what would happen, in similar conditions, to the 32-foot *Fidelio* with an inexperienced crew of one?

Morning Cloud was a new boat, the third *Morning Cloud*, built with a hull of cold-moulded mahogany that is immensely strong. She was fully equipped with fittings and navigational equipment of top quality.

During the last week of August she was racing at Burnham-on-Crouch, which is north of the Thames Estuary. At the conclusion of the races she headed back to her home port of Cowes on the Isle of Wight. The crew of seven was under the command of Don Blewett. With the exception of the prime minister's godson, Christopher Chadd, all the other members of the crew were thoroughly experienced sailors and had crewed on similar deliveries of the two previous *Morning Cloud*s.

The 1:55 shipping forecast on 2 September predicted for the Isle of Wight sea area "southerly winds Force 6 to gale Force 8, locally severe gale Force 9, veering southwest with periods of heavy rain." This was a reasonably accurate forecast. At the Royal Sovereign light tower, about twenty miles east of Shoreham, an average force of 10 was recorded. This, of course, is the mean force. In the gusts it must have attained Force 11 to 12 and possibly much higher. Force 12, it should be remembered, is 64 knots (74 miles per hour), where hurricane force winds begin.

The wind must have approached these higher limits even on shore, because trees and signs suffered extensive damage. In Shoreham's eastern harbor where *Fidelio* was berthed, inside the locks where no waves or swells from the outer harbor can reach, water was being picked up off the surface and blown away in sheets of spume.

At 6:30 P.M. *Morning Cloud* was just opposite Shoreham (it was still light, so I probably could have spotted her had I known she was out there then), steering for the Owers Light Tower. The weather was deteriorating so

Blewett ordered the main to be reefed still further and the storm jib set.

At dusk, the Owers Light was sighted. By now the wind had risen to forty-five knots as measured by their anemometer. In the violent gusts which characterized this weather front the force was much higher. Nonetheless, *Morning Cloud* continued to make progress toward the west in spite of the tumultuous seas, which is testimony to the seaworthiness of the modern ocean-racing yacht.

At 10:00 P.M. the watch was relieved by Nigel Cumming and Gardner Sorum, two veteran ocean-racing sailors. A little later Gerry Smith, from the other watch, joined them and lay down on the weather side of the cabin.

At about 11:00 P.M. a huge wave threw *Morning Cloud* onto her beam ends. She righted quickly and Gerry Smith could see Sorum thrashing in the water astern, held to the boat by his lifeline. Smith yelled for help, and Bob Taylor and Barry Kenilworth rushed out on deck. It took them several minutes to get Sorum back on board. Then they realized that Cumming was missing. When he went overboard his lifeline had parted and he was nowhere to be seen.

Meanwhile, Don Blewett had stayed below to start the engine, which would help them tack the boat as they searched for Cumming. Almost immediately it packed up. Four men stayed on deck looking for Cumming while Blewett assessed the damage below. Several of the laminated deck beams had been split and water was standing a foot above the cabin sole. First, he attempted to send out a distress signal on the radio transmitter, but it wasn't working. Then he got out flares and fired one after another. The first two failed to ignite while the third one was immediately blown away horizontally by the savage wind and fell into the water.

At this point Christopher Chadd opened the companionway hatch. He stepped out into the cockpit and his shipmates noticed that he wasn't wearing his safety harness. They yelled for him to get it just as another great wave hit the yacht, capsizing her to a point that the mast dipped below the surface of the sea. This wave also broke the catch securing the foreward hatch and water poured below through both open hatches. After laying over on her side for what semed like a long time, she suddenly righted.

The wave or the sudden capsize catapulted Chadd overboard where he could be seen about twenty yards from the boat. Taylor tried to free a lifebuoy to throw to him but it was fouled in a tangle of gear and could not be freed. Efforts were then made to throw him a line, but by then he too had disappeared amid the raging waves.

Down below, water now stood about three feet over the cabin sole. Worse still, all but one of the remaining five men on the boat were seriously injured. Blewett had broken his shoulder and three ribs, one of which punctured his lung. Sorum's right arm was broken in three places and he also had three broken ribs. Smith had cracked one vertebra and displaced three others.

This, then, was the situation when Blewett decided to abandon ship. The six-man raft had been lost when the cockpit lockers flew open during the first knockdown.

However, the four-man raft remained and was successfully inflated and launched. Even then, the injured men had no difficulty boarding it, since by now *Morning Cloud* was so low in the water that the raft floated at deck level.

Five men in a four-man raft was no disadvantage since the extra weight seemed to act as ballast and helped the raft remain upright. Most of the survivors were seasick, which, very likely, was caused by their injuries and shock rather than by the motion of the raft. Not the least surprising aspect of the *Morning Cloud* saga is that all five survivors survived the raft ride despite their injuries and being capsized when the raft entered the area of breaking surf at Brighton Beach.

They landed at 7:30 A.M., at about the same time I walked over to the shore at Shoreham to observe the state of the sea. Huge breakers marched in from the Channel and crashed, one after another, on the beach with unbelievable ferocity. While the beach at Brighton is not as steep as it is at Shoreham, I could only wonder that these exhausted and injured men managed to land safely in such a furious storm.

All this has made a vivid impression on me, and I vow to wear my safety harness and hook on whenever I go out on deck if there is any motion at all.

Noon—Hot, sunny, still a mirror-like sky and Channel. I decide to have lunch in absolute silence so I turn off the engine and make iced tea, salad, and a ham sandwich. I can still see the Owers Tower, which marks the position of dangerous reefs that have devoured hundreds of ships.

The same placid sea and weather prevailed here on

the morning of August 5, 1588. I could visualize the mighty Spanish Armada in its crescent-shaped formation drifting along on the east-setting tidal current. Their left wing was just about where *Fidelio* drifts over an empty sea. The center and right wing stretched out into the Channel, where Drake and Howard with the main English fleet were harassing them. Between the Spanish left and the Owers shoal was an English squadron led by Frobisher in the *Triumph*. As a breeze came up, the Spanish left, under the command of Captain General Medina Sidonia in the great galleon *San Martín*, attacked Frobisher's squadron. The English, who were well aware of the nearby dangerous shoal, slipped around the end of the Spanish line, with the exception of the *Triumph*, which was cut off. Frobisher promptly lowered his boats and began to tow her away. Other English ships saw his predicament and sent their boats to help. Then the wind freshened. Frobisher cast off the lines and sailed away to rejoin his squadron.

Meanwhile, Drake had stepped up his attack on the right tip of the crescent, and the Armada gradually worked its way to the northeast, or right toward the Owers shoal. However, the pilot who stood next to Medina Sidonia on the poop deck of the *San Martín* was an experienced coastal navigator, and he recognized the danger signs of shoaling water just in time. The flagship signaled the fleet to come about and stood away to the southeast. The fleet followed, avoiding destruction by a matter of minutes. The attempt of the wily Drake to drive the Armada onto the treacherous Owers reef had very nearly succeeded.

From here the Armada sailed on up channel, constantly shadowed by the English with their faster ships and longer range guns.

After lunch I fire up the motor, pass the Nab Tower, and still no wind.

5:00 P.M.—Still dead calm, unprecedented for the notorious English Channel. I'm tired of steering so I again shut off the motor and settle for a mug of sherry followed by a salad-and-spaghetti dinner, in a setting of dinner music and breathtaking sunset. Finally at 7:00 P.M. I can see a vigorous-appearing cat's-paw skipping up channel toward us. Quickly I hoist the mainsail and the number-two jib. Under sail at last! I tie the tiller amidship and engage the Hydrovane self-steering gear. It seems to work perfectly, which is a big relief.

By 9:00 P.M. the current is setting us closer to the long string of lights on the Isle of Wight, so I alter course. The wind is increasing and during the next hour I make several sail changes and roll down more and more of the mainsail, work that goes slowly in the dark, due to lack of practice before setting out. I only had time, after all, for one afternoon of sailing before today. Also, I must keep a close watch on the lights of various ships all around us. In the dark, with poor visibility, it is almost impossible to judge their courses. It gives me an unpleasant feeling of vulnerability and helplessness.

11:00 P.M.—I light the Tilley lamp and tie it to the handrail in front of the mast where it shines on both the jib and mainsail. A chilling southwest wind whistles up the Channel. I'm glad to go below and write up the log. Five minutes later I check topside and freeze when I see, two or three points off the starboard bow, a brilliantly lighted passenger ship less than a half mile away and on what appears to be a collision course. At this point the ship should have been turning to port to pass astern of *Fidelio,* but there is no sign of any such evasive action.

My mind barely functions as I watch the rushing ship loom larger and larger. Now the ship clearly doesn't have time to turn. At the last minute I unlash the tiller (the tiller is lashed amidship when the self-steering gear is in use), and swing it hard to starboard, ease the sheets, and run off downwind. The ship, course unchanged, thunders past less than one hundred yards from us. As its lights recede in the darkness, I'm shivering from cold and the close call. After a while I recover enough to resume course. Before this night of nightmares ends, two more near misses appreciably reduce my life expectancy.

The Near-Fatal
Race

God motivates all life and directs His undivided and ceaseless attention to every part of creation from the great spheres of light and cauldrons of energy to the tiniest flower unfolding its petals upon the earth. —ALBERT EINSTEIN

SEPTEMBER 15TH: The second day out of Shoreham my main problem is staying awake. As the afternoon blows away—we are beating hard to windward—I get more sleepy by the minute. However, I am awake enough to review my errors in strategy, due not only to inexperience but also to my arrogant stupidity.

My plan was to head directly out to the separation zone* in midchannel, i.e., safely in between the one thou-

* There is a north lane for ships going down the Channel, a south lane for ships going up Channel.

sand ships passing up and down the Channel each day, then proceed directly down Channel to the open Atlantic. What I failed to take into account was the large number of ships *crossing* the Channel that must pass through the separation zone.

Nor did I consider the large number of fishing boats that are likely to be encountered any and every place in the crowded Channel. And these, of course, must be carefully avoided even by vessels under sail. This makes it impossible for a singlehander to sleep even in the daytime. In short, a singlehander must either make short hops from harbor to harbor during the day (as the English do) or else take a crew and drop them off at Plymouth or Falmouth.

Also, if I had listened to my English friends I wouldn't be starting so late in the season. A small boat like *Fidelio* should not be crossing the Bay of Biscay this late. Some insurance companies won't insure a boat that leaves England after August.

To try to stay awake another night (or two, or three?) would turn into a game of Russian roulette. As the sun sets I alter course for Weymouth, which is tucked behind the Bill of Portland and its notorious tidal race.

The entrance channel is well marked, since it also leads to the Portland naval base and is used by the British navy, but I have trouble recognizing buoys and leading marks in the dark. After motoring endlessly, often in circles, I finally locate the picturesque harbor of Weymouth, where yachts are rafted several deep along the quays on both sides of the harbor. I tie up to one of them and collapse. It is 3:00 A.M. on the sixteenth of September, my fifty-sixth birthday.

SEPTEMBER 16TH: At 8:00 A.M. I climb over the sev-
ral boats rafted inside *Fidelio,* walk into town, and carry
back my groceries, including freshly baked bread. After a
lunch of fried rice and still-warm bread, I climb the hill to
the coast guard station, which commands a sweeping view
of the Portland naval base, the Bill, and the race beyond
it. I tell the man on duty I'm heading down Channel tomorrow and ask the best time to pass through the channel
between the race and the West Shambles buoy. He replies
with great authority, "Be there at 7:00 A.M."

SEPTEMBER 17TH: The morning dawns cloudless,
with another mirror-flat sea. At 7:00 A.M. after motoring
for an hour and a half, I can see the buoy in the distance.
The water is no longer calm. On the contrary, it's getting
rougher and rougher. Off to starboard, in the center of the
race, I can see frothy breakers splashing skyward. Is this
normal at slack water? Now I can see the buoy being
thrown about by violent, chaotic seas. I know I should
turn back, but if I can make the last hundred yards to the
buoy I can turn the corner enough to run with the current
and still miss the reef.

Suddenly poor *Fidelio* is being thrown about like a
bottle at the bottom of Niagara Falls. The Portland Bill
lighthouse, remote, detached, stands etched against the
northern sky. Now the waves are frantic like those in the
eye of a hurricane. Hanging on to the lashed down boom
with both hands, the tiller between my knees, I can barely
stay in the cockpit.

Above the sound of the swirling water I hear a heart-
rending sound from the engine, a grinding, clanking
sound. It is still running but delivering no power, at least

not enough to compete with the madly rushing current. We start drifting and tossing out of control backwards toward the deadly Shambles shoal! I can do nothing but pray. We miss the reef with a few feet to spare, then limp back to Weymouth on one cylinder.

The engine has thrown a rod. By the time I find a new one in London and find a Volvo diesel mechanic to install it, ten days have passed. Then a few gales delay us; it is that time of year.

OCTOBER 1ST: Finally, a fine day. This time I pass between the Shambles lightship and the West Shambles buoy, far from the race, a considerable detour but also much safer. When I pass close to the lightship, the crew wave to me with V signals.

In the afternoon the wind freshens and veers more into the southwest. The chop gets steeper and the ride rougher beating to windward, but no problems. Until, that is, after an early dinner, which includes salad followed by fried potatoes, onions, and peppers. I need a pail of water for the dishes. Holding on to the guardrail with my left hand I drop the bucket with my right, while holding on to the lanyard. Just as I do so a big wave hits us on the quarter behind me.

The impact wrenches me loose. I fall backward, twisting, and my lower back hits the concrete edge of the cockpit. I end up stunned, with head and shoulders halfway down the companionway stairs. No bones appear to be broken, but when I finally get up, the pain in my back is intense every time I bend over or raise my left leg to take a step.

I can't understand how this has happened, since I am

careful and not accident prone. Lower-back problems are old friends of mine and I know from experience that this one will get much worse before it gets better. I must return to Weymouth as fast as I can. So I wear the ship around, ease the sheets, hoping I can make it back before being completely immobilized.

We make it back, in a cold drizzle, by 3:00 A.M., but only with the indispensable help of two powerful pain-killers. For several days I am flat on my back. Happily, the mate of the *Lucy Q*, which I am rafted against, is an angel who takes care of me until I am once again ambulatory.

OCTOBER 7TH: During these days I lie in my bunk thinking. From the very beginning I have suffered one setback after another. Is someone trying to tell me something? Am I stubbornly set on having my will prevail over that of a higher power? I pray for guidance and I meditate. When I finally become more recollected an inner voice tells me to carry on. Now I feel at peace and I also feel an inner certainty that this venture will be a success.

Francis Chichester and his wife, Sheila, believed implicitly in the power of prayer and with good reason. He had been stricken with lung cancer. Five specialists agreed it would prove fatal unless he submitted to surgery at once. The fact that he was too weak to get out of bed suggested they might be right. Nonetheless, he refused to have the operation. Instead, his wife and friends prayed for him. According to medical experts, what happened was impossible. He began to recover and was soon up and working on *Gypsy Moth 4*, which had just been delivered from the builders. He overcame apparently insurmountable difficulties in preparing for sea, then embarked on the singlehanded circumnavigation of the world that made history.

Since the dawn of history the wisest men and women that the human race has produced have agreed that prayer is the most powerful force available to man. Augustine Baker said, "Prayer is the most perfect and the most divine action that a rational soul is capable of. It is, of all actions and duties, the most indispensably necessary."

Why is this so? Because prayer concentrates the mind, and anything can be achieved by the perfectly concentrated mind/spirit. Prayer is beneficial even if you do not believe in a supernatural response to it. The evidence is overwhelming that positive thinking, which is what prayer is, can indeed cure illness both mental and physical. The mind can regulate any of the bodily functions, such as the immune system, blood pressure, heart rate, and so on. In short, mind creates and controls matter, not vice versa.

The long hours confined to my bunk have been fruitful ones. They have enabled me to back off and view things more objectively. While going through the outward rituals that lead to self-realization, I am actually suffering inner disquietude (or fear?), not to mention lower-back pain. Why? What has gone wrong? Aldous Huxley analyzes the problem and presents the solution.

"Disquietude is caused by anxiety and too much concern over the future welfare of the individualized ego. This results not only in moral evil and the mental sufferings which moral evil inflicts, in one way or another, but also in certain characteristically human derangements of the body." He then goes on to enumerate the long list of bodily ills that are caused by stress, preoccupation with self, and failure to believe that mind/spirit heals and keeps the body healthy.

The solution, Huxley says, is to lose ourselves in prayer and God. "The highest prayer is the most passive. Inevitably, for the less there is of self, the more there is of God. And the more there is of God the more our personal suffering and problems are diminished."

Carl Jung, the famous physician and psychiatrist, had this to say about the source, prevention, and cure of mental and bodily suffering: "I have treated many hundreds of patients, the larger number Protestants, a smaller number Jews and not more than five or six believing Catholics. . . . There has not been one whose problem in the last resort was not that of finding a religious outlook on life. It is safe to say that every one of them fell ill because he had lost that faith, which the living religions of every age have given their followers, and none of them has really been healed who did not regain his religious outlook."

This emphatic statement by a scientist is all the more remarkable in that it dates back to a period when belief in the psychosomatic origin of illness was by no means as generally accepted as it is today. Certainly, at a time when it was confidently believed that scientific discoveries would eventually eliminate disease, a majority of Jung's colleagues rejected out of hand the proposition that it is just as rational to believe in miracles as to believe in antibiotics.

Yet we know, based on the testimony of doctors, that

people with apparently incurable maladies have, in fact, been cured in an incomprehensible manner for which the doctor could offer no explanation other than the direct intervention of God, i.e., the power of mind/spirit over body.

While the agnostic and the atheist will ridicule any such explanation, the believer knows that in either event the cure is attributable to God, whether it is outwardly and apparently due to faith and prayer—or to antibiotics.

If all the foregoing has any merit, then what I need to do is to spend more time meditating and concentrating my mind on curing this back problem.

OCTOBER 9TH: Almost overnight I'm near normal and ready to go. The 1:55 P.M. shipping forecast is the best in some time. Force 5 to 7 from the northwest with showers.

6:30 P.M.—My fourth assault on the English Channel begins with a new plan of action based on the advice of the local fishermen I should have sought out and listened to in the first place. Namely, to pass *between* the race and the Bill of Portland. Fishermen wisely avoid the West Shambles buoy area.

As we pass the naval base and round the Bill I keep one hundred yards from shore as the fishermen advised. No problems. Then we head into Lyme Bay in order to stay well away from the race. A nasty night looms with gusty winds and drizzle. There will be no sleep. For one thing, there are science-fiction–like firework displays all around us, brilliant flares and red-lighted helicopters darting about, which I presume come from the British navy at play. According to the chart this is a submarine maneuvering area. Later I spot several stationary ships brightly lighted, one after another dead ahead. Factory ships of a fishing fleet?

Lyme Bay seems to be as crowded tonight as it was one evening nearly four hundred years ago, when the Spanish Armada made its second contact with the British navy. The first skirmish had occurred off Plymouth with each fleet testing out the other. The heavier gunned, faster, and more weatherly English ships circled the unfamiliar crescent formation, firing from too great a distance to do any real damage. In contrast, the great ships of the Armada attempted to close and board the enemy but without any success.

As darkness descended the Armada rounded Start Point and sailed into Lyme Bay. Drake, who was vice-admiral of the English fleet, was leading the pursuit in *Revenge,* which displayed a stern lantern to guide the rest of the English fleet led by his commander Lord Admiral Howard in *Ark Royal.* In the middle of the night Drake doused his lantern and turned off course without signaling this move to his commander. Farther out in the Channel was the Spanish galleon *Nuestra Señora del Rosario,* which had been disabled the day before in a collision with another Spanish ship. Drake was famous for his ability to home in on rich treasure ships and, as it turned out, the *Rosario* was the richest one in the Armada. There were more than 50,000 gold pieces in Captain Pedro's strongchest plus much other booty. While the *Rosario* was disabled so that she could not sail efficiently, she was still in perfect fighting trim. Yet so great was Drake's reputation, among the Spanish, for superhuman ability, that when

Captain Pedro identified his assailant as Drake's ship the *Revenge,* he surrendered his larger, stronger ship without firing a shot.

Meanwhile, Howard, after losing sight of Drake's light, soon sighted another one that he assumed was Drake's and which he followed the rest of the night. By now he had outrun the bulk of the English fleet and there were only two other ships with him. At dawn, off Berry Point, he saw before him the entire Armada—no less than 128 ships—but no sign of Drake. The three English ships beat a hasty retreat and finally found the main English fleet, which Drake had by now rejoined.

The English squadrons now intercepted the Armada just off Portland Bill, and the greatest sea battle the world had seen up to then took place, as the two fleets drifted before a southeast wind back into Lyme Bay. This second battle was also indecisive with no mortal wounds being inflicted as the combatants continued to feel each other out and improvise battle plans to meet the new and unfamiliar tactics of the other side. Finally, when the wind backed into the west the Armada resumed its plodding course up Channel. The English fleet headed toward its nearby bases to replenish its supplies of powder and cannonballs.

Neither the English nor Spanish contemporaries of Sir Francis Drake and Captain Don Pedro criticized their behavior. Yet Admiral Howard had specifically instructed his captains to ignore the *Rosario* and pursue the enemy. Drake not only disobeyed the order but endangered the safety of the English fleet by doing so. Don Pedro had surrendered one of the Armada's most powerful ships without any resistance to an inferior opponent. Certainly today both would have been court-martialed and dismissed from the service in disgrace for their respective roles. What a change in discipline since Elizabethan days. For better or worse?

OCTOBER 10TH: At 5:30 A.M. I can see the Berry Point light and two hours later the Start Point light. By 3:00 P.M. we are about fifteen miles south of Salcombe when a black, evil-looking squall bears down on us. I drop the jib and heave to under the reefed mainsail, with the helm lashed down drifting at a speed of about one knot to the southwest. A second squall passes through; after that I expect a letup which does not materialize.

The thought of spending a gale-torn night out here chills me even more than the wind blowing down from the Arctic. The omnipresent steamers are what worry me. They seem attracted to small sailboats like iron to a magnet. And no matter what I do, in this weather *Fidelio* will still be invisible from the deck of a big ship.

Reluctantly, I decide to seek shelter in Salcombe. First I read the directions for entering—they sound complicated—then fire up the engine and head north. For ten minutes we smash into waves, fall off waves and make little, if any, progress.

Since I fear the worst this is what happens. A piercing sound of metal insanely grinding and vibrating. From the cockpit I can look right down on the engine. The universal joint is acting like a jumping jack. The drive shaft bends out of alignment as I watch it. I switch off the engine, then heave to.

Two half-inch bolts securing the engine to its bed

have sheared off. Really this seems impossible when you consider that the breaking strain of a half-inch stainless-steel bolt is more than 30,000 pounds. One consolation: With the engine out of order I won't have to steer any longer, a chore I detest.

The wind continues to howl all night with no letup. Ships seem to be everywhere, so when the black night envelops us, I light the Tilley, crawl cautiously up the deck, and lash it in front of the mast. Then, since cooking is out of the question, I eat a handful of raisins and climb into my bunk with oilies still on as protection against various leaks.

Capsize!

The sea is at its best at London, near midnight, when you are sitting before a glowing fire. —H. M. TOMLINSON

OCTOBER 11TH: By 5:00 A.M. the wind and sea have subsided noticeably so I get under way. Estimated position twenty miles south of Start Point. This has to be the day to escape from the prison of the English Channel, and what an Indian summer day it turns out to be. By noon we are well past Start Point. In the distance I glimpse the Eddystone lighthouse, or do I imagine it?

I spend a couple of hours upside down over the engine trying to figure some way to rebolt it and straighten out the propeller shaft. The engine itself runs fine, which means I can charge the batteries, but it won't turn the prop, at least not smoothly enough to use.

Should I put into Falmouth for repairs? Intuitively I know that if I turn back now I'll never start again, at least not this year. True, by now it's much too late in the season to be crossing the Bay of Biscay in a 32-foot boat. The Bay has a reputation for dangerous storms at this time of year that are only equaled in these latitudes by the Tasman Sea. But something more important than my physical safety is at stake. If I throw in the towel now, my battle to conquer fear will be lost forever. Repair the engine? Just an excuse to chicken out. The engine means nothing once we are out in the Bay of Biscay and in the Atlantic.

2:00 P.M.—We are opposite the reef with the sinister name—the Manacles. Its ugly name has been repeatedly justified over the years. At high tide the extensive rocks of the Manacles are nearly submerged. At low tide I could see them plainly from Pendennis Point in Falmouth, where I practiced celestial navigation.

The outer rocks are almost a mile from shore, so it is not surprising that well over one hundred ships rounding the Lizard and heading for Falmouth have selected the Manacles as their final resting place. A much smaller number have embraced these horrors while leaving Falmouth, probably because more skippers prudently choose to leave port only when the weather is reasonably good. Moreover, when leaving they know where they are and where the Manacles are. When returning they may not.

Then, too, there were a few ill-starred ships that were neither entering nor leaving Falmouth and were still lured to their destruction on the Manacles as if by some evil genie. The most sensational and inexplicable of these was the luxurious and ultramodern liner *Mohegan,* which departed from London on October 13, 1898, bound for New York. On the following day at 2:40 P.M. she passed Start Point and signaled, requesting that her progress be reported to the owners, the Atlantic Transport Company of London.

At 7:00 P.M. the *Mohegan* plowed, at her top speed of fourteen knots, into the Manacles with an impact that ripped out a good part of her bottom and flooded most of her eight watertight compartments. Within ten minutes she was resting on the bottom with only the tip of her funnel showing above the water. The reason for the disaster was never discovered. The captain and all of the officers perished with the ship, as did another hundred passengers and crew members.

Adverse weather played no part in the disaster. Although it was dark, visibility was excellent, sea and wind moderate. Several people on shore clearly watched the liner closing the Manacles, her lights blazing. At the coast guard station they had time to fire off warning rockets and flares before she struck. Yet, according to the few survivors, no effort that they could see was made to slow the ship or avoid the reefs.

The official court of inquiry concluded that the captain must have ordered the wrong course by accident or neglect. Moreover, none of the officers had noticed the mistake even though the lights of Falmouth must have been conspicuously visible off to the right. According to survivors, at no time did the two lookouts or the second officer who had the watch indicate that there was any cause for alarm.

I submit that this is simply beyond belief. There must be some other explanation for the tragedy. I have just sailed from Start Point to the Lizard, although I passed the former farther off than did the *Mohegan.* The compass bearing that was fixed in my mind was the one from Start Point to the Lizard: 255°. In short, I knew in my sleep that I must steer 250°, or even more to the south, depending on where I was in relation to the rhumb line, to clear the Lizard. If the captain, in a moment of blackout or while drunk, ordered a course of 270°, wouldn't the second officer question it? Of course he would.

A more logical explanation is that the compass went haywire. And even this is not good enough. No navigator relies solely on the compass, especially not when approaching the Lizard! Moreover, both the Lizard and Falmouth lights must have been visible. At this moment I can look out and, despite the brilliant sunlit day, plainly see the flashes of the Lizard light. How much more prominent these lights would be on a dark night and from the protected deck of an ocean liner thirty or forty feet above my position.

My own guess is that the *Mohegan* was deliberately wrecked. The facts, at least to the extent that we know them, permit no other explanation. The officers in on the plot may have anticipated beaching her with no loss of life and then miscalculated the position of the Manacles. Or, perhaps, the captain had some grudge against the company and deliberately put her on the Manacles. Or again, maybe he had personal problems and chose this macabre way of solving them. We shall never know.

4:00 P.M.—This has to be the most thrilling day of my life: sailing out of the English Channel into the Atlantic Ocean. The famous Lizard lighthouse is about two miles off the starboard bow. The weather is perfect, sunny, smooth, blue seas and a perfect sailing breeze, like a yachting painting by Monet. Two graceful shearwaters keep pace with *Fidelio*, about ten feet behind us and fifteen feet above the surface of the sea.

I think of all my predecessors who sailed past the Lizard, from Francis Drake to Francis Chichester. What were their thoughts when they saw the Lizard? Did they wonder, as I do, if we are all pawns on a giant chessboard? Did they realize, as I will someday, that *everything* that happens to us is for the best?

For example, here I am making a dream come true as a direct result of events that, at the time they occurred, I considered to be catastrophic. We only know in retrospect what course of action is in our best interest.

My feeling of euphoria subsides somewhat when I tune in the shipping forecast: Force 8 predicted for tonight. However, by now I'm reconciled to the prospect of gales. I may as well get used to them so I don't even consider running for shelter as I would have a couple of days ago.

By 6:00 P.M. we are about five miles west of the lighthouse. The wind is now Force 6, gusting to 7, conditions *Fidelio* revels in as she flies along on the starboard tack still carrying the working jib and the mainsail slightly reefed.

I'm pleased to see that the self-steering gear manages without any difficulty.

I'm below at the stove browning some meat for chili. Without any warning I'm thrown against the stove. I'm startled and then realize that I am on top of the stove! Though dazed I manage to turn it off and dimly realize that I am looking at solid green water through the cabin window. Books, cushions, and gear of all sorts rain down from the starboard seats and lockers, which are overhead.

Fidelio has been knocked down!

Instinctively, I scramble out into the cockpit, forgetting to hook on my safety harness. The mast and sails are almost in the water, held down by the wind, which now must be blowing at Force 7 or 8, a full gale. First I let the sheets fly, then crawl up the starboard cabin side to the mast, release the halyards and, with an exhausting effort, pull in the mainsail little by little. *Fidelio* has already righted herself. Now for the jib, which is flogging fearfully. I release its halyard, making sure it has a turn around the winch on the mast, then scramble forward and pull down the sail, releasing just enough of the halyard to permit the sail to come down. If too much is freed it will become entangled in something aloft.

After securing the sails I crawl back to the cockpit, shivering from cold and shock, wondering what has happened. Of course, when the wind jumped from Force 6 to 7 or 8, it meant that we were overcanvassed. But it is the sea, not the wind, that capsizes a sailboat; and at this moment the seas, though steep and close together, are not more than eight to ten feet high. I can only assume that the yacht fell off one of those occasional waves that tower two to three times the height of the average wave,* just as a powerful gust from a new direction hit the sails. Clearly, in the future I must be more vigilant and reduce sail sooner, even if this means our speed will suffer.

Midnight—*Fidelio* rides fairly comfortably with eight rolls in the main, the storm jib backed and tiller lashed down, forereaching at about one knot toward the west. However, in the gusts the jib flogs badly so I hand it. Thereafter, we make a little more headway without the jib acting as a brake, which is fine because we want as much westing as possible.

Periodically, I take bearings on the Lizard light and the loom of the Land's End light, checking for any change in the wind. As long as it holds in the northeast we are drifting out into the Atlantic with no lee shore worries. So far I am luckier than the thousands of sailing ships that were wrecked on the inhospitable shores behind us, victims of southwest gales.

I go below and view the wrecked cabin with distaste. However, cleaning up now is out of the question; it's all I can do to sit up and write, let alone move about using my hands for anything except holding on. Besides I'm still shaken up, scared, and depressed.

Meanwhile, a continual line of ships parades past,

---

* It has been calculated that one wave in twenty will exceed twice the height of the average wave and one in one thousand will exceed three times the average height. Anyone who gazes out across the ocean week after week will confirm these statistics. One or two of these "freak" or "rogue" waves are nearly always visible. Subsequently, I also learned that in the sea area between Land's End and the Lizard, instantaneous, 180° changes in wind direction are not unusual.

ensuring another sleepless night. However, unlike the previous nights, none seem intent upon running us down. The reason is that we are at the outer reaches of Mount's Bay, about five to seven miles from the Lizard and fifteen to seventeen miles from Land's End. In short, we are well inside (or north of) the shipping lanes around these two famous (or infamous) headlands. All mariners want to round them with plenty of sea room to spare because they are acutely aware of the thousands of ships that have foundered on or near these deadly capes.

Mount's Bay was a potential deathtrap for sailing ships because weather and wind could change with bewildering rapidity, as I have just learned. And no matter what the wind direction, these sudden changes could, and all too often did, force sailing vessels on to a lee shore from which they never returned.

When the wind reaches hurricane force, which does happen in these waters but fortunately not often, even motor vessels can suffer the same fate as sailing vessels, especially if they are steaming in ballast. Such casualties are not a matter of ancient history. Within the past ten years a variety of ships, ranging from the *Torrey Canyon* to freighters and trawlers—all equipped with modern electronic navigational gear—have been lost in these waters, sometimes without leaving a trace.

From where we are right now (if it was daytime) I could see where hundreds of proud ships of every description, · including those in the Spanish Armada, were wrecked. Most of them must have sailed close to my present position, and I can imagine, all too vividly, how those sailors must have felt as they were blown toward destruction. Among these I can recall an uncanny series of events that ended in a twin shipwreck off the Lizard.

In May 1872 two barques hailing from Genoa, the *Marianna,* seven hundred tons, and the *Nuovo Raffaelino,* two hundred tons, sailed from Bassein, Burma, bound for Falmouth for orders. Both carried cargoes of rice and, as was usual in the days of sail when time of arrival was uncertain, they were to call first at Falmouth to find out where to deliver the rice.

A few days after sailing they parted and did not see each other for the next three months. Quite by accident they met again off the Isles of Scilly, some forty miles due west of my present position. On the twentieth of September they again lost sight of each other when a dense fog enveloped them. The following afternoon both ships crashed onto the reefs off the Lizard, not far apart but without being aware of the presence of the other. Both crews got safely to shore and both ships were total losses when the wet, swelling rice burst them apart.

OCTOBER 12TH: Fortunately, as the new day dawns, the gale-force winds and rough seas diminish somewhat, permitting us to get under way at 9:00 A.M. Off to the right the Wolf Rock lighthouse is just visible. This lonely and dangerous rock rises out of the deep water eight miles southwest of Land's End. It was not named Wolf because of its predatory nature, although it consumed many victims before the lighthouse was built, but rather because the long, immense Atlantic swells funneling through an opening in the rock produce a wolf-like howling sound.

In 1861, a famous lighthouse designer of the day, James Douglass, was commissioned by Trinity House to construct a lighthouse on the rock. He arrived in July with the necessary men and material to do the job, and, evidently, with full appreciation of the difficulties involved. At any rate, the men were accompanied by their families and this was fortunate, because the job stretched out for ten years before it was completed.

It is a heavenly day. The shearwaters, gulls and other sea birds, which I can't identify, glide effortlessly back and forth behind us. I breathe a sigh of relief. At last we are out of the nerve-racking English Channel.

To the north I still get an occasional glimpse of the Wolf Rock lighthouse. This will be my last sight of land for how many days?

Ships are in sight most of the time for we still are in or close to the various shipping lanes, which converge on the Bishop Rock,* the goal of all ships passing from the Atlantic into the English Channel. At 2:00 P.M. a Russian freighter approaches on a collision course but turns in plenty of time to pass astern of *Fidelio*. The crew wave to me in a friendly fashion despite—or because of—the conspicuous American flag we are flying.

The yacht is moving well in eight- to ten-foot seas, occasionally rolling the lee rail under. The chart table is on the starboard side. I am seated at it, plotting our position, when a sizable spray of water drips onto my head and runs down my neck. I inspect the outside of the hull and find that the toe rail has pulled away from the hull, probably caused by one of the breaking waves that smashed the boat during last night's gale. Evidently, I

---

* The southwesternmost part of the Isles of Scilly.

failed to caulk properly some bolt holes underneath the toe rail, and the force of a wave hitting up against it causes a miniature jet of water to spurt through above my seat.

At 10:00 P.M. I can see another squall line ahead, so I reduce sail, which causes no reduction in speed, a sure sign that the wind is building up. A series of squalls keeps me awake most of the night but precipitates no other problems.

Visions and Signs

Life is mystical because everything in it has a second dimension which is God. He walks unrecognized among us every day, everywhere. Alas, we no longer recognize Him because in our arrogance we think we no longer need Him. —The Breviary

OCTOBER 13TH: One hour of sleep a night is not enough. At dawn I'm weak and weary. Slowly I hoist myself into the cockpit after having my usual breakfast of tea and oatmeal. The slate-black sea has changed to pale oyster shell. With a sense of awe I watch the darkness become shimmering, pale green light. I open my Breviary to the thirteenth day of the month. The first verse seems uncannily appropriate.

> *We feel Thy calm at evening's hour.*
> *Thy grandeur in the march of night;*

And when the morning breaks in power
We hear Thy word, "Let there be light."

My Breviary has been a great consolation in recent years. It has helped prevent me from getting too high when things were going my way and too low when they weren't. For this I thank Father Stephen Boylan, who was the first prior of the only Carthusian monastery in America, the Charterhouse of the Transfiguration. Before meeting him I had no idea what a Breviary was. Nor had I ever heard of this most austere order of contemplative monks.

Although I have only met Father Boylan once, we have corresponded for many years and developed a true guru-devotee relationship. Certainly that one meeting changed my life. He obviously existed in a different world of joy and bliss than the world I was living in.

On that visit he took me into his own small private chapel, where a shaft of sunlight glowed on the granite altar. He turned, touched me on the shoulder, and said, with tears in his eyes, "Paradise is here now! Oh, if troubled people in the world only realized that! God is waiting to shower his grace on them if they will only turn to Him to receive it."

After that meeting I realized that I was searching for that inner serenity he had found, only I was searching in the wrong places and in the wrong way. Then and there, I decided to seek God more and Mammon less.

It's uncanny how I sense his presence here on *Fidelio* this very moment. And perhaps he is here! Really. After all, he is a far, far advanced spiritual master; many such masters are reputed to be able to make bodily appearances in distant places. Perhaps if I was sufficiently far advanced on the path to perfect mind concentration, I would be able to *see* him with my own eyes.

There are many records of gurus who have materialized their bodies in the presence of favored devotees, staying and talking to them for hours. In these encounters the master's body is actually ethereal because it exists in a different dimension of space/time. But it appears to be real to the devotee just as a person on a television screen appears lifelike.

Suddenly, I laugh out loud. The irony of it! I would be the least likely person in the world to embrace a life that required getting up twice in the middle of the night to go into an unheated church and pray. Well, I now get up several times a night to go out on a cold, wet, heaving deck, where I very often do some praying.

Perhaps Father Boylan has more to do with my being out here than I realize!

OCTOBER 14TH: The wind has subsided to a perfect sailing breeze. But not for long. By noon we are almost becalmed and I should hoist the genoa, but I'm too lazy. Instead I take the noon sight.

Observed altitude	33° 00′	90°		56° 48′
Corr: Sun and Dip	+ 12′	−33° 12′	dec	07° 44′
	33° 12′	56° 48′	lat	49° 04′N

That's how simple getting your latitude is. Take the sun's angle with the sextant and add or subtract the sun's declination (north or south of the equator), which is given at two-hour intervals in the nautical almanac. I won't reproduce the longitude calculations, which are more complicated but which can be mastered by anyone who can take a sextant sight and can also add and subtract.

Despite my slothfulness, the noon-to-noon run works out to be a respectable eighty-five miles. Cheered up by this showing I drag the genoa up on deck and hoist it. This show of energy naturally produces a calm. I should take advantage of it to get some sleep. Instead, fascinated, I watch the world beneath us, which becomes clearly visible for the first time.

One large brown sea turtle is guarded by seven red-and-black-striped pilot fish which follow his every twist and turn as if being pulled by a magnet. A fat little brown fish lazily swims into and out of our shadow. Nine incredibly gorgeous dorados circle us like jet fighters in formation. What colors—electric blue to green with char-treuse-colored tails and fins.*

Sleepy as I am a voice says, "Meditate." So I go up on the foredeck, which for the first time is almost stationary, and sit in the lotus position with my back against the cabin front. I gaze for a while at the sea endlessly undu-lating away, seeking the distant mist-hidden horizon. Then I am (without conscious effort on my part) trans-posed to another world, another level of consciousness. I am no longer me. I am no longer aware of my "self" or of my body.

A powerful force literally pulls me out of this life and this world. I am terrified and feel like a person at the end of a rope hanging over a bottomless chasm. I want to resist

---

* The dorados—later on there were only eight—stayed with us for more than a month. I don't recall any other voyagers reporting similar long-term escorts. Were they watching over us in some way?

this force but I am powerless, helpless. I am racked by great sobs; suffocating tears run down my cheeks and chin, dripping down on my shirt.

I don't know how long this goes on but eventually the worst of the fear of surrendering to this powerful force subsides and I seem to dissolve in a sea of light, of love; wave after wave of pure love sweeps over me. Am I crying tears of joy or sorrow? Both, because this state of consciousness is beyond joy or sorrow. All questions are answered, all doubts are resolved. Or rather, questions and doubts no longer exist or have any meaning.

I would welcome death if it would enable me to remain forever in this state of unfamiliar but perfect bliss, a sort of complete detachment from the ties that bind us to time, the world, and the body. Time is suspended. I cease to exist. The "I, me, mine" is replaced by something timeless and immortal.

Gradually I return to a normal state of consciousness, utterly drained of any physical energy.

This placid day's sailing over a relatively calm sea is followed by what seems to be developing into a pattern: a wild sleepless night. By 10:00 P.M. there are squalls all around, and all of them seem to contain plenty of wind. Also, lots of fishing boats around; clearly, the edge of the continental shelf is a good place to fish. They have the right of way and I constantly alter course to avoid them. I marvel that they venture forth day after day, year after year for, perhaps, an entire lifetime. A tough breed of men if the way I feel right now is any criterion. It's going to be a long night.

The Ghostly Pilot

O lost, and by the wind grieved, ghost, come back again.

—THOMAS WOLFE

OCTOBER 15TH: The rainy, squally weather continues all morning. Later, when it has moderated, in a bemused state I continue to jog along with only the storm jib up; meditation is fine, but sailing comes first out here. So I return to my sea world, hoist the genoa, then relax with my pipe and admire the graceful sea birds that are following *Fidelio*. White with black outlines and two black marks on the throat. They are not pictured in my bird book.

3:00 P.M.—The now-placid sea reveals an undulating swell composed of hills of water, perhaps two cables (a cables is 100 fathoms or 600 feet) between crests and a hollow in between as large as a square city block. This accounts for the rough, turbulent conditions last night. While I am contemplating the silent, empty ocean, two reports that sound like cannon and quite close make me jump. I grab the binoculars and sweep the horizon 360°. I can see nothing. There are mysterious happenings here as well as in the Bermuda Triangle.

Probably the sea is such a mysterious, wondrous realm to us because we are land mammals trespassing in an alien world—frightening at times, enchanting at times, the mysterious secret that is always tantalizingly just beyond our grasp. The land-bound laws of causality don't apply out here. Events don't happen; they simply *are*. Intellectually, I measure my progress in hours and days; an ingrained fifty-six-year habit. But the new me repudiates those land-based habits. The new me yearns to remain here forever in the forever-now moment.

Being becalmed, the bane of most sailors, enchants me, as does eating dinner in softly glowing candlelight while listening to a concert being broadcast from London. Thank goodness for the BBC and the Mozart piano concerto they are playing. Which one is it? I am familiar with all of them because I once owned a complete set of tapes featuring Lili Kraus. Now, in another world, I listen to music composed by a man who must be considered one of the supreme geniuses of the human race. Yet, he was a humble man, who considered his genius to be a gift from God and a responsibility that drove him to work at a pace no human could endure. He was only thirty-five when he died. Most of the great creative geniuses did not claim personal credit for their masterworks, which they felt originated not in their minds but rather from some outside source.

The luminous perfection of Mozart's music does, indeed, seem to be beyond the abilities of any mere mortal. Was this music born from the one-pointed concentration of Mozart's mind? From the intervention of some master composer in the spirit world? Or from both?

The purpose of art, poetry, literature, and music is not to entertain or divert us; it is to show us a glimpse of the worlds beyond our five senses. The arts do this by at least partially cleansing the windows of perception. In this context W. B. Yeats said, "The purpose of poetry is to prolong the moment of contemplation, which is the one moment of creation when the mind, liberated from the bondage of the will, reaches out to the 'infinite.'" According to T. S. Eliot, "Poetry is not a turning loose of emotion but an escape from emotion; it is not the expression of personality but an escape from personality." These goals are precisely those of every spiritual aspirant.

By 8:30 P.M. the wind has returned, and we are flying along under the storm jib and deep-reefed main. I lie on the weather side of the cabin top beside the companionway, ready to drop the sails at the first sign of being overpowered. The low clouds rush by, almost touching the mast like a scene in a Gothic novel.

Although the yacht is hard-pressed and several times we narrowly escape a knockdown, I stubbornly hold on. Fatigue impairs my judgment. Only an hour or so of sleep a day is beginning to tell. By 11:30 P.M., in a semidazed state, I realize that things are getting out of control. I manage to get the mainsail down and secure without changing course, which is 235° with the wind from the north, i.e., abaft the beam.

In retrospect, what happens this night appears quite impossible and I have no explanation for it. With the mainsail lashed to the boom I go directly below, forgetting to lower the storm jib. Nor do I disengage the self-steering or lash the helm down to heave the boat to. I simply don't think about these things.

During the first weeks of the voyage I never felt alone and never felt lonely. I wasn't alone on the boat, for I had company. Either some member of my family, Father Boylan, or English friends—Ian Kingsley-Brown, Eric Swift, Martin Pennington—were present. I knew I was physically alone but they, nonetheless, were with me all the time. This is difficult to explain.

But the night of the fifteenth of October was different. The seas were immense and *Fidelio* took a fearful beating from them. The gale continued all night and *Fidelio* held her course of 235° all night. Never before or after was I able to get the yacht to steer herself with only a single headsail set! There was no way that *Fidelio*, unaided, could have stayed on course. The wind vane will not steer the boat with just the jib set.

It was nothing short of miraculous considering the chaotic conditions of that night. She should have broached to in five minutes or less. I had also foolishly left out the companionway washboard and stood in the cabin looking out into the cockpit. Someone was steering the boat for me! Of this I was absolutely certain! I felt no anxiety or fear at all, after those previous nights when I had been filled with both. Occasionally, I sat down, braced in the seat, and smoked my pipe. But most of the time I stood, gripping the handrails, staring out at the cockpit which was dimly but clearly lit by the orange compass light, striving to focus on whoever was there. I could see no one. At least no visible physical form.

Was a higher power helping me? A master mariner of the spirit world? There have been innumerable stories or claims about such inexplicable interventions on land as well as at sea. I especially remember reading about the help received one night by Joshua Slocum, the first man to sail alone around the world. His experience was quite similar to mine. I must confess that my logical mind has always viewed such claims with skepticism. But no longer. This is the only way I can account for the events of this extraordinary night.

OCTOBER 16TH: The early light reveals an angry sea. However, as the sun rises the wind subsides somewhat. I come out of my trance and cook a big pan of oatmeal topped with several spoonfuls of brown sugar. On deck again, I see a freighter approaching off the starboard bow. It alters course, passes close astern, and when a cable or so away, someone shouts through a hailer: "Big waves coming." "Big waves coming." Not a very encouraging greeting. Nonetheless, I wave my appreciation for their thoughtfulness in so advising me.

As usual the wind increases as the sun sets. After handing the big jib and before hoisting the storm jib in anticipation of the night's festivities, I eat dinner in relative comfort and am pleased to note that the self-steering gear holds the boat on course with only the mainsail set. While eating I can hear and feel something bumping and scraping against the hull; then I hear voice-like squeaking sounds. It turns out to be a school of porpoises playing games with *Fidelio*. The rotor on the log also seems to fascinate them so I haul it in for safekeeping. At times they scrape against the hull with sufficient force to alter our course by some five to ten degrees.

I head for the bow to hoist the storm jib when a vicious squall sweeps over us. After one look at the seas I drop the main. The "big waves coming" have arrived. *Fidelio*, lying ahull, scares the life out of me. She slides down the face of a mountain, decelerates like an elevator coming to a stop, rolls over to leeward until the toe rail is under water and I am sure she won't recover, then rolls back almost as far to windward.

In my bunk I hold on, fearing the violent jerks will pull out the hooks above the bunk that anchor the "leeboard," actually made of canvas. Finally, I move the mattress and make up a bed on the cabin sole. Then, discouraged, I write in the log: "At the moment we have completed the first full week of the voyage, with four nights of gales and two days becalmed. At this rate I will run out of food and water before reaching the latitude of the Canaries."

Once again a full gale pounds us, at least so it seems, judging from the sound of the wind and the violent motion of the yacht. However, by now I am beginning to feel at home in my dice box, so much so that I am determined to get some uninterrupted sleep. I even undress for the first time since leaving, and climb into my down sleeping bag. Luxury! I'm quite comfortable and secure on the floor wedged between sailbags. I fall into a deep sleep.

Sometime later I awake with a start, so paralyzed with sudden fright that I can't move. I distinctly hear heavy footsteps on the deck overhead. It sounds like two or three people. My first thought is that we have collided with another boat and the crew have boarded *Fidelio*. So either the other yacht or *Fidelio* must be sinking. By now I am totally awake but in complete darkness. The kerosene lamp in the cabin is out and so is the Tilley outside on the deck.

I grope for the torch which I always place close at hand but I can't find it. Instead, I locate my pants and frantically try to put them on. After some frustrating, agonizing minutes I pull them on and push back the companionway hatch. It's lighter outside. The white froth and foam throw a ghostly light over the jagged seascape. There is no one on deck, nor can I see another boat. What a relief! After a while I close the hatch, locate the torch, and fill and light the lamp. I sit down and light my pipe, still shaky from this all-too-real fright, then fill a mug with sherry and drink to my guardian angels.

Did I have a nightmare? Hallucinations? I don't know. But I do know that fatigue is becoming a major problem. Why was I so intent on getting my pants on? Why didn't I switch on the cabin lights?

Finally, I struggle into foul-weather gear and safety harness, go out and get the Tilley and relight it. The new quartz chronometer advises me that it is 4:00 A.M.

OCTOBER 17TH: By noon the wind seems to have less weight behind it. The seas are enormous but not steep and close together as in the channel. I decide to give it a try and hoist the storm jib and deep-reefed main. We fly away like a roller coaster up and down the mountainous waves, which are much too long to slow us down. But housekeeping presents problems. I go below and boil water for a cup of hot chocolate. Just as I start to drink it a lurch splashes it all over the cabin, while I am thrown down on a box containing cartons of eggs. I have visions of an enormous omelette and I am not disappointed when I open the box.

3:00 P.M.—Still lots of wind plus a huge swell from the north fighting, at times, with waves from the west that are still high and steep enough to earn my continuing respect. When the two meet at a certain angle the yacht would broach to if I didn't take over from the Hydrovane and steer at an angle of about twenty degrees down the swell.

5:00 P.M.—Damn it to hell! The batteries need charging and the motor refuses to start. I would like to eat dinner and turn in but the masthead and compass lights are essential at night. This usually means air has gotten into the fuel line and must be bled out, a job I don't like. It takes me the best part of an hour to do it.

When I finish it still won't start. Then I think to look at the plug that covers the exhaust outlet. A good guess: Our latest gale dislodged it and, as a result, the exhaust pipe is full of water, a condition that can ruin a diesel engine. I drain the water out and turn the ignition key. It starts! Whew! I was worried.

6:00 P.M.—I decide to celebrate by drinking the last of the sherry before preparing dinner. I only brought two bottles and now I wish I had ten cases stored in the bilge. Twenty years ago I started drinking to obliterate the despair that threatened to overwhelm me. It helped then but

I've been drinking too much ever since. A bad habit that I couldn't conquer ashore. Well, after studying the chart I calculate the nearest bodega is in La Coruña, Spain, 150 miles southeast of us; get thee behind me, Satan.

The chaos continues to mount when my dinner is thrown off the stove onto the cabin sole. After cleaning everything up I now have a backup dinner right at hand. In a short time I am eating my giant omelette.

At 8:00 P.M. I look out to check the course. We are headed 160°—straight for Spain. I alter the sheets and self-steering to 200°. The wind has eased and this turns out to be the first good night's sailing since leaving England. Orion dead ahead, Polaris astern. A lovely clear night—a night of countless brilliant stars, which reminds me of the two things that most impressed Kant: "The moral law within, the starry sky above." The vast canopy overhead makes me marvel at the insignificance of man-kind, in contrast to his feeling of importance, of being the center of the universe. How foolish and arrogant when you consider that our galaxy, the Milky Way that spreads across the sky above me, contains about one hundred thousand million (100,000,000,000) individual stars, i.e., suns similar to ours. The diameter of our galaxy is about 100,000 light-years or, stated differently, 600,000,000,000,-000,000 miles. Quite a distance! But this only represents our local community. Beyond our Milky Way about a thousand million galaxies can easily be seen by the two-hundred-inch telescope on Mount Palomar. This means that if these galaxies contain, on the average, as many stars as ours, we can "see" perhaps 100,000,000,000,000,000,-

000,000 individual stars or suns. If only one percent have planetary systems such as ours it would still be quite a few (strike out the last two zeros above). This truly boggles the mind.

If all of these hundreds of billions of stars are radiating energy at the same rate as our sun (and bear in mind that all heat and energy we receive here on earth are only a tiny fraction of that constantly being emitted by the sun), it is in accordance with Einstein's formula $E=MC^2$. That is to say, the energy latent in matter is equivalent to its mass times the velocity of light squared. This is why the sun, which converts hydrogen into helium plus energy (as does the hydrogen bomb), can last billions of years—all the while radiating huge amounts of energy. Many scientists believe that this cycle of the universe is dependent on the continuous creation of hydrogen. How? By whom?

Einstein came to believe that it is not possible to distinguish between mind and matter. In short, the physical explanation of the universe must be sought in the spiritual, rather than the material, realm. And Sir James Jeans, back in 1929, concluded in *The Universe Around Us*,

> Traveling as far back in time as we can brings us not to the creation of the picture but rather to its edge; the creation of the picture lies as much outside the picture as the artist is outside his canvas. Therefore, discussing the creation of the universe in terms of time and space is like trying to discover the artist and act of painting by going to the edge of the picture. This brings us very close to those philosophical sys-

tems which regard the universe as a thought in the mind of its Creator, thereby reducing all discussions of material creation to futility.

Jeans also concluded, "The stream of knowledge is heading toward a non-mechanical reality; the universe begins to look more like a great thought than like a great machine."

Midnight—As usual I check the chronometer against the BBC time signal in London. When Big Ben strikes twelve it is exactly midnight. The chronometer has been losing one quarter of a second per day. The secret of accurate navigation is accurate time.

Cape Finisterre

No yacht, however sound, and no crew, however experienced, are immune from the dangers of the sea.
—Heavy Weather Sailing

OCTOBER 18TH: A radio-direction-finder (RDF) fix places Cape Finisterre about 110 miles distant, bearing 160°. This closely agrees with my dead-reckoning position, which, in turn, indicates that my celestial navigation has been right on. This cheers me up no end. I taught myself while in England and had never taken a sight at sea before leaving Weymouth.

The 1:55 P.M. shipping forecast predicts Force 6 to 7 for Finisterre. But a Spanish broadcast, if I heard it correctly, forecasts, *"Fuerza de ocho o nueve."* In any event, I decide I have succumbed to fatigue and lethargy long enough, so I break out the plywood covers for the cabin windows. I spend a wet, miserable hour screwing them into place.

I also fit the portable bilge pump on the deck outlet and the spare on the cabin-floor outlet with its discharge going into the sink. I also put extra lashings on the life raft and the dinghy, which fits upside down between the mast and the companionway hatch. Now I am ready for the worst, which, judging from the mare's tails far aloft, might be approaching.

By 10:00 P.M. the foam-crested waves sweep relentlessly out of the black night, some breaking over the yacht, hurrying along the deck, into and almost filling the cockpit. When *Fidelio*, driving ahead, falls off a wave the sails empty, then refill with a force that threatens to dismast us. I wonder how the sails and self-steering gear withstand the assault. I can't stand it even if the ship can. So I go through the now-familiar drill (even in the dark) of heaving to under bare poles, remove the wind vane to the safety of the cabin, lash the tiller down, and lay ahull.

By 1:00 A.M. we are being smashed in an unbelievable fashion. Occasionally, the shock is so great that it snuffs out the candle, the sudden motion being equivalent to blowing it out. One such time catches me standing in front of the stove (strapped in) brewing some tea. My head hits against the cabin carline, cutting my left ear and forehead.

According to my dead-reckoning position, when we hove to we were about ninety-five miles off the northwest coast of Spain, toward which we are now drifting. This seems to be an ample margin of safety even if the gale lasts two or three days. From time to time, angry seas break with sledgehammer force against the cabin side (the sound is literally like a sledgehammer hitting) and, I'm sure, would have smashed unprotected windows. Either fatigue or familiarity with gales has gained the upper hand; securely tied in my dripping bunk I am able to doze off and on until dawn.

OCTOBER 19TH: Finally the clock tells me that it should be light outside (with the covers over the windows the cabin remains dark). Cautiously, I pull back the hatch and peer out at an awesome spectacle. It reminds me of an Alpine winter landscape: mountainous waves with foam-crested peaks being blown off horizontally in streamers of spray as far as the eye can see. The motion has definitely become more violent and a new octave has been added to the unearthly whining of the wind tearing at the mast and rigging.

I calculate the average wave height at twenty-five feet with some towering thirty-five feet. The feeling of our motion is unmistakably like hitting an air pocket when flying. Again *Fidelio* slides down a wave, rolling until the lee rail is under, then a big one follows and she skids along almost going over. This is frightening.

For the first time I notice water lapping up to the floorboards around the battery box, which is under the companionway stairs. With water sweeping over the entire boat small amounts come in everywhere, but especially through the stern hatch when the transom is periodically submerged. I start pumping it into the sink. Each time the cockpit fills, the yacht seems to be definitely more waterlogged and down by the stern.

This worries me, but I am thankful for the steel bridge deck separating the cockpit and cabin. Without it we might not survive this onslaught. I am also thankful I had the foresight to make the plywood storm windows, and for the extra heavy shrouds and stays; not to mention the strongbacks I built across the cabin top to reinforce it and the mast against just such sledgehammer blows as are now battering us.

However, I am by no means complacent about the situation. From time to time rogue waves break near *Fidelio*. If one caught us just right, it would unquestionably roll us all the way over. I installed rigging sufficiently strong to survive such an eventuality, but I fervently pray that we won't have to undergo such a test. By now I'm convinced that lying ahull is a dangerous tactic, but we are still being blown toward the rockbound coast of Spain so there is no alternative.

There are two 1½–inch drain outlets in the cockpit floor. I thought that these were plenty large enough. But it is disturbing to see how long it takes for the cockpit to empty. One reason that had not occurred to me while on dry land is that once full, the stern of the boat is submerged to such an extent that the cockpit drain outlets are far enough below the water to prevent them draining and, I suspect, at times water might even be flowing into the cockpit through the drains.

Two five-gallon (imperial) jerry cans of water and one of diesel fuel are stored in the cockpit because there wasn't any other place to put them. Clearly, our buoyancy would be greatly improved if these were empty rather than full. All at once I realize that immediate physical survival is the all-important consideration! So I struggle into deck gear and harness, climb into the cockpit, and dribble out the oil over the weather side, hoping it will calm the seas. It does where the oily slick streams out behind us, but not where we are. I also empty the two cans of water over the side and relash the empty cans in the cockpit. This gives us added buoyancy when the cockpit fills. Will I regret the lost water? Probably, but better to survive now and worry about that later.

This weather creates a problem that reminds me of Professor Babbit's class in sanitary engineering (see "The Psychology of Solitude"). Actually, the only time I use the head is when *Fidelio* is in a harbor or marina, so I haven't used it once since leaving Weymouth. Instead, I use it to house sailbags. The most convenient toilet is a bucket, ordinarily located in the cockpit. However, in weather like this it wouldn't be safe (or dry) out there. After using it inside, the contents must be carried out and consigned to the deep, which requires the greatest care and concentration, like running an obstacle course carrying a sackful of eggs. So far I have avoided any spills!

The 1:55 P.M. shipping forecast catches up with the elements at last. It predicts Force 8 to severe gale Force 9 for the Finisterre area. Well, I am where it is happening and can testify to the general accuracy of their forecast. However, it should not be assumed that the wind blows evenly over an entire area. It varies over surprisingly short distances. If it averages Force 9 this might mean it varies from Force 7 to Force 11 in contiguous sectors of the area.

As the afternoon slowly blows away, I become increasingly apprehensive about the safety of the yacht lying ahull under these deteriorating conditions. The snowstorm outside looks even worse than this morning. Only Force 10 could produce such a landscape; at least what I see looks like the photos of Force-10 seas in *Heavy Weather Sailing.* A caveat is in order, since all sailors tend to overestimate the wind force.

I not only pray but I also concentrate my mind on giving *Fidelio* the extra buoyancy and stability needed to keep her from rolling all the way over. Then I turn to the Breviary.

He that dwelleth in the secret place of the Most High shall abide under the shadow of the Almightly.
—Psalm 91

I'm reminded of this psalm after pondering one of today's entries:

"There is a part of the soul untouched by time and flesh, which is completely spiritual. There God is perpetually verdant and flowering with all the joy and glory that are in Him. Here God glows and burns without ceasing, in all His fullness, sweetness, and rapture. To be united with God in this part of the soul is to be ageless."

You can believe without *really* believing. Now I do. In this secret part of the soul you are secure against *any* adverse events or conditions. I no longer am filled with fear, rather with a calm feeling of inner peace. If I survive, so be it; if I don't survive, so be it.

By now I'm certain that *Fidelio* will sink if rolled over. There are just too many places where water comes in, the result of my inability to properly fasten the wood cabin to the ferrocement deck. Also, water would pour in through and around the loose-fitting companionway hatch.

6:00 P.M.—For the first time the stove is thrown off its tight-fitting gimbals onto the cabin sole. An hour later a wave breaks right on top of the companionway hatch and water pours down into the cabin. I think that the end is at hand and cry out loud, "This is it!" The clanking and smashing of the self-steering gear as the seas crash against the transom or against the hull and cabin side combine with the shrieking wind to create what sounds like a soundtrack from hell.

I feel helpless, completely at the mercy of the implacable sea. We slide down the face of these two- and three-story waves like an elevator, with the same feeling of weightlessness, expecting at any minute to be rolled all the way over. I promise myself, "If I survive this and reach land safely, never again will I leave it." *Fidelio* comes back from the point of no return again and again.

I'm fearful that my guardian angel may be getting as tired of this as I am. It's about time I try to help myself. The wind has been slowly veering from west to north so that we are no longer being driven toward a lee shore. I recall how Joshua Slocum had survived an ultimate storm off Cape Horn by running downwind with the storm jib sheeted flat amidship. I decide to try it.

First, I hook two safety lines onto my harness, crawl up the deck pushing the coiled jib sheet ahead of me, pass it back inside the shrouds, then through the genoa track block to the winch. Then I repeat the process with the other sheet. Next I drag the storm jib up to the foredeck, which is scooping up green water from time to time, hank it on, hoist it, then scramble back to winch it in as fast as possible, first on one side, then the other, until the tack of the sail is exactly amidship and only inches from the mast. I lash the tiller amidship. *Fidelio* falls off and runs downwind. The motion moderates and she shows no tendency to broach to, even with the tiller unattended. When a wave breaks on the quarter, throwing her off the dead downwind course, the storm jib, rigid as plywood, immediately brings her back on course.

This fifth long night of waiting out a gale proves to be much more comfortable and less nerve-racking than the others. The contrast with lying ahull is startling. What a relief. Never again will I lie ahull in a gale, providing I am not off a lee shore. Avoiding the latter eventuality will always have the highest priority.

OCTOBER 20TH: During the night the wind veers a little farther and by 11:00 A.M. I estimate that we have drifted sixty to seventy miles due south, which places us northwest of Cape Finisterre and about thirty miles off. However, an RDF fix places us only twenty miles off, which suggests a current set us toward the Spanish coast.

The wind eases somewhat and since I want to make all the offing possible, I decide to get under way. I reroute the jib sheets, hoist the main, which is already deeply reefed, and steer southwest away from land. This requires a major effort with *Fidelio* rolling heavily in the still monumental seas. Once under way, I take over the steering; it would be too much for the Hydrovane, up one side of the mountain and surfing down the other side. It's more like skiing than sailing.

By 6:00 P.M. I am once again exhausted. Fortunately, the wind and seas finally have subsided somewhat, so that I can once again let the self-steering take control. I heave the boat to, bring up the wind vane, slide it into its slots, screw it in place securely, and remove the pin that locks the rudder in a fore and aft position. I move the vane from side to side to make sure the self-steering rudder responds properly.

My heart skips a beat. I discover the rudder is gone! Let this be a bad dream from which I will soon awake. If not, this is the final, devastating blow. This has to be the absolute low point of the voyage. I have no spare rudder and improvising a replacement seems out of the question. I decide to have a good dinner, a good sleep, and think about this problem in the morning even if it does mean still another night of no progress.

OCTOBER 21ST: Most of the morning I ponder the dilemma of replacing the missing self-steering rudder. Apparently, either the bolt holding the rudder to the one-inch stainless-steel shaft had worked itself out or the glass-fiber rudder had fractured under the repeated sledgehammer blows as we lay ahull. In either event, the rudder now lies some 15,000 feet below us in Davy Jones's locker. Maybe he can make use of it. Next to broken bones or being dismasted, this is the setback I had most feared—proving once again that what you most fear is what will happen: Fear must act like a magnet. Naturally I have two spare wind vanes but no spare rudder.

Now the hope of making a nonstop passage from England to the West Indies seems shattered. I decide to lay a course for the Canaries, where I will phone the Hydrovane people in England and have a new rudder flown out.

Meanwhile, the Canaries are still a long way off, over a thousand miles. Perhaps ten days if I had self-steering, maybe twenty days if I steer twelve hours a day and allow twelve hours for eating, sleeping, and navigating. Clearly, I must make every effort to get *Fidelio* to steer herself without the Hydrovane.

I am hunched over the tiller in the misty rain, thinking about various self-steering ideas, but I don't get a chance to test them. A gale force squall blows in from the west and I barely drop the sails in time. By midafternoon the wind has risen to gale force, luckily from the north. I resheet the storm jib flat and drift downwind.

This turns out to be the sixth night (out of twelve) spent hove to in a gale, which must constitute some sort of record. Once again *Fidelio* suffers and groans under the onslaught. Water comes in everywhere until it seems as though I'm living in a cold shower. Everything is soaking wet, books as well. The gale continues all day and begins to moderate as twilight descends; most unusual. I make no attempt to get under way. Instead, I settle for what I hope will be the first uninterrupted sleep of the voyage.

OCTOBER 22ND: The seas this morning are enormous, evidently due to the unusually large swell rolling down from the north—the result, I presume, of an even more severe storm in the Bay of Biscay, a good place not to be.

While eating dinner, I notice that the seat of my

pants is wet. I had put on a dry pair when I came in. The foam-rubber cushion is soaking wet. More water has run down the side of the hull from the toe-rail leak than I had realized. In addition, food supplies, such as cereal, macaroni, and the like, stored in the locker under the seat are also drenched, with most of it already mouldy. Another reason to head for the Canaries.

Death Versus Life

The world at its best isn't miserable, isn't hateful—it is mad. The pursuit of worldly pleasures and ambitions as ends in themselves is madness, because it disregards the real purpose of life, which is to know God in ourselves and in other people.

—SWAMI VIVEKANANDA

The life of prayer is also a life of mortification, of dying to self, it cannot be otherwise; for the more there is of self, the less there is of God.
—ALDOUS HUXLEY

OCTOBER 23RD: I'm getting used to sleeping through gales or near gales. When I wake up the sea is relatively calm, about time, so I spend an hour hanging over the transom trying to figure out some way to jury rig a new self-steering rudder. The problem is that I am not mechanically inclined. In contrast, I'm sure my English friends, Eric or Martin, could devise something in short order.

Well, at least I must try. I have plenty of plywood under the bunk mattresses, plus glue, so laminating and shaping a plywood rudder should be relatively simple. I also have antifouling paint. The problem is finding a one-inch shaft four feet in length, then rigidly attaching the rudder to it. A hole would have to be drilled in the shaft to receive a quarter-inch stainless-steel bolt (which I have plenty of) that locks it into the Hydrovane gearbox.

First, I think of the propeller shaft, which is now useless. I could unbolt it from the universal joint and push it far enough down into the packing gland to permit plugging the opening into the boat. Then I could dive under the boat, attach a line to the shaft and propeller, pull the shaft free of its strut, then pull them aboard. I'm pondering the pros and cons of this scheme when I remember I would have to drill a hole through the solid one-inch bronze shaft with only a hand-operated drill. It would take days, if I could do it at all.

Then I think of a better idea. The stern pulpit is made of one-inch hollow stainless-steel tubing. When I installed the Hydrovane I had to cut out the top horizontal section to permit the wind vane to rotate freely. I saved this section (as I save everything else). How long is it? It takes a while but I finally find and measure it. Three and one-half feet: six inches too short. I doubt that this matters. The self-steering rudder was three feet long, so that one foot of the shaft protruded above the top of the rudder to engage the gearbox, which the wind vane activates. That means this new shaft will have only 2½ feet attached to the rudder, which doesn't seem critical. Also drilling a hole in this tubing poses no problem. I'm optimistic as I start to work.

5:00 P.M.—A long day's work. The new rudder is cut out and laminated—a layer of quarter-inch marine plywood sandwiched between two layers of half-inch material, glued and clamped. Now it must set for twenty-four hours.

After dinner I lie on the forward bunk and ponder: Millions of people all over the world will recognize yesterday as the anniversary of the day John F. Kennedy died. How many are aware that Aldous Huxley died on that very same day? Ten? One hundred? Probably not many more. How is this possible since Aldous was far and away the greater man?

Of course, my opinion is not altogether objective since Aldous helped me, at least indirectly, recover from a state of acute crisis in my life. It was twenty years ago when I had the good fortune to meet him in Santa Barbara, where I was trying desperately to make my first business a success. At times it seemed certain that it would fail and I would walk the country lanes at night sick with worry about what the future held for my young children. In due course, these worries took their toll and I was on the verge of collapse.

What is the cure for a nervous breakdown? Before answering this question we must first ask what a nervous breakdown is and why it occurs. Isn't it the result of undue preoccupation with and anxiety about our personal and selfish interests? When we can think of nothing but ourselves, or those who represent extensions of our own egos, then worry and anxiety follow as surely as night follows day. When these fears and uncertainties reach an intolerable level, we refer to our condition as a "nervous breakdown." At this stage a person is truly living in hell.

This neglect of the spirit adversely affects the body. In my case, in addition to severe depression, it was manifested in a series of physical symptoms, ranging from insomnia to dangerously high blood pressure and a heart murmur. All of these things were, of course, psychosomatic in origin.

I was soon under a doctor's care. This made matters worse rather than better. After a few weeks on a diet of rauwolfia, tranquilizers, and sleeping pills, I was ill not only mentally but also physically, and desperate enough to try anything. I was at such a low ebb that I was even willing to entertain the idea (subconsciously) that the only cure lay in following a spiritual road back to good health.

One day a friend who knew of my admiration for Aldous Huxley invited me to go to a Vedanta Society meeting where Huxley was to speak. I had only a vague idea of what Vedanta was, but I quickly accepted in the hope of meeting Huxley, the author of the brilliant, satirical novels that I so much admired. I didn't realize that by then he had repudiated or advanced beyond that phase of his career.

Aldous transformed me from a cynical agnostic into a sincere devotee and spiritual aspirant. After all, if one of the outstanding minds of the century could, in all humility, turn to faith, God, prayer, contemplation, and all the rest, then maybe it wasn't all a lot of superstitious nonsense fit only for those who could not think for themselves. Until then I was proud to be a militant atheist, which is why, of course, I had a nervous breakdown. This, then, is how I began to overcome pride, the pride that kills spirit.

The encouragement Aldous gave me, as well as his book *The Perennial Philosophy,* cured and converted me.

Converted me to what?

At last I began to appreciate the urgent necessity to get in tune with the powerful intelligence and force that creates and maintains a hundred million galaxies, each of which contains a hundred million stars like our sun! When we get in tune with this power we can achieve a higher level of consciousness so superior to our everyday "normal" consciousness that it cannot begin to be described in any earthly language. When we are plugged into this superpowerful force our abilities, even on the temporal level, are multiplied and we become capable of achieving anything we are capable of conceiving.

OCTOBER 24TH: Yesterday I shaped the new rudder, using sharp chisels and a Surform shaver. The trailing edge narrows down to about one-half inch. I gouge out a half-inch half circle from the leading edge, which will receive the shaft. After chiseling it out roughly, a couple of hours with the wood rasp reduces it to a rough approximation of a hollow half circle in the plywood edge of the rudder.

I have two small tubes of epoxy glue, not nearly enough to do the job. So I will use it plus the urea-based glue I used to laminate the stringers and plywood cabin top. Now I smear glue on the hollowed-out edge and on the shaft, then on the inside of a piece of one-eighth inch aluminum sheet metal that I have been saving for just such an eventuality. The shaft fits reasonably close into the hollowed-out edge of the rudder. I wrap the aluminum sheet tightly around the shaft, then bend it flat along either side of the rudder. Numerous ring nails hold it in place. This too must set for twenty-four hours.

I survey my handiwork with satisfaction. It should work if the glue holds in water and also if it will bond stainless steel with aluminum and wood. We shall see.

OCTOBER 25TH: While waiting for the glue to set, I try various combinations of twin headsails in an attempt to get the boat to steer herself. After several hours all I achieve is a large dose of frustration.

5:00 P.M.—The shaft and rudder seem to be firmly bonded so I lower the boarding ladder over the transom. By kneeling on the lowest rung I can slip the rudder shaft up in the sleeve that receives it without any problem, then bolt it in place. So far so good.

Next I attach the wind vane. When I swivel it, the new rudder reacts as it should, so I hoist the sails, set the course, tie the tiller amidship, and once again the Hydrovane does the steering. I'm filled to overflowing with euphoria and gratitude, also disbelief in what I have accomplished. This calls for a celebration dinner. The menu: canned grapefruit, followed by salmon grilled in lemon-butter sauce, potatoes pan-browned in butter, spinach, and rice pudding for desert.

11:00 P.M.—I'm asleep when a motion change awakens me. She has broached to. Sails flap but it's no big deal (a preventer line running from the boom end through a block at the forestay fitting and back to the cockpit prevents the boom swinging across in an involuntary gybe or broach to). The first thing I check is the new steering rudder, and I could cry at what I find. The shaft has come unglued! Already? The new rudder would now be on the sea bottom if I hadn't rigged a safety lanyard. I untie the lanyard, let the rudder drop off the shaft, then haul it aboard. Three days' work down the drain.

The wind is still out of the north so I wearily begin the storm jib drill. At least we will be making some progress in the right direction while I'm asleep.

OCTOBER 26TH: For two days now I have been trying to get *Fidelio* to steer herself with twin headsails. The trouble is mine aren't twins. The different sizes make it impossible to exert equal pressure on the tiller (via shock cord to the sheets). Finally, I give up disgusted and discouraged. Nor can I think of any way to solve the steering rudder problem.

OCTOBER 27TH: I wake at dawn, probably due to the lack of motion. Both wind and ocean are calm. The eastern sky looks like the beginning of the world, calm and silent with misty, multicolored castles towering above the invisible horizon.

I sit down to contemplate this enchanting, mystical vision of Paradise. Automatically I do my yoga breathing. Then I close my eyes and see the vision in my mind's eye. Between two castles I see a shaft of beatific light that transforms the surrounding castle clouds into a billowing sea of absolute bliss. The clouds dissolve into a sea of celestial light, a sea of pure cosmic consciousness in which "my Father and I are one." United forever. Nothing else will ever matter.

When I finally return to the concrete world of *Fidelio,* I force myself to turn on the radio and prepare a hearty breakfast. Otherwise, in that mood I fear I could succumb to an irresistible urge to walk toward those distant castles where God seemed to be calling me to join Him in Paradise.

The remainder of the day I seem to alternate between this world and that other world, which is our true home. I have always thought that suicide was the result of extreme despair, but now I'm sure that it can also result from a state of consuming joy. The mystics of India assure us that ordinary people who experience *samadhi,* i.e., union with God, will not continue to live unless they have a role to fulfill in this world that forces them to cling to this life. Now I understand what they mean.

I suspect that this may account for the disappearance of some singlehanded sailors from Joshua Slocum to Donald Crowhurst. In short, death is not something to be feared but rather something to be welcomed, as many people demonstrate at the time of their death. Sri Ramakrishna died of cancer in 1886 and suffered great pain during the final month. However, much of the time he was in a state of *samadhi.* In this state the pain was replaced by the indescribable joy and bliss of union with God. On the last day, surrounded by his disciples, he radiated joy and serenity.

Similarly, Aldous Huxley died of the same type of cancer, and according to his wife he greeted the end joyfully and serenely in a state closely associated with *samadhi,* although the state was induced, in part at least, by drugs.

Another example: Carl Jung suffered a severe heart attack in 1944 when he was sixty-eight. Near death, he had a remarkable vision. He was floating in outer space, looking down on the bluish globe of the earth (this was twenty-five years before astronauts brought back photographs that looked exactly as the earth did in his vision). Nearby was an asteroid with a temple on it. He was about to enter it and die when his doctors revived him because, as they told him, he was needed back on earth. The last thing he wanted was to return to the world and all its problems. Subsequently, he almost hated the doctors who had interfered with his dying.

After regaining his health he wrote: "What happens after death is so unspeakably glorious that our imagination and feelings do not suffice to form even an approximate conception of it." He also wrote to one of his students who was dying of cancer: "The difficult part is to get rid of the body, to renounce the crazy will to live, in order to experience the beginning of one's truly real life with everything you were meant to be and never reached. It is something ineffably grand."

In short, the experience of death might be compared to that of a person who has been confined to a dungeon all his life; then suddenly, he finds himself on a mountaintop. The irritations of his jail life and the problems of mankind suddenly mean nothing in comparison with the vista that now lies before him.

Furthermore, I now know for certain that the message of eastern avatars and the Christian mystics is true: that *samadhi,* or the kingdom of heaven, is attainable in this life—at any time. Nothing in this life matters except attaining this goal at the earliest possible time. All else is folly.

The Moonbow

*In the month of November 1872, 180 of the sailing ships leaving
New England ports never returned (including the* Marie Celeste).
—Mysteries of the Sea

OCTOBER 28TH: The wind remains out of the north so
I try a different tactic—running wing and wing. The
genoa is poled out on one side, the full main on the other
side. This is the answer, as long as I steer. Again I try
leading the sheets through blocks to the tiller in an effort
to get the yacht to steer herself. No luck. Another day
mostly wasted.

Moreover, my hands are so sore from handling sails
and ropes that I can hardly hold on to anything. By now
three separate layers of skin have peeled off, probably due
to the constant immersion in salt water. It's a magical

night with moonlight shimmering on and reflecting off the restless, dancing waves. Also, the air has become noticeably warmer, and for the first time I leave the companionway hatch open all night. I steer until I can no longer stay awake.*

This evening we are close to the position where the mysterious brigantine *Marie Celeste* was discovered sailing along with no one aboard her. She was sailing on the port tack with all sails filled by a breeze from the north. Her headsails, however, were aback and she was heading up and falling off as though no one was at the helm, which, of course, was the case if the sworn testimony of Captain Morehouse of the American brig *Dei Gratia* is to be believed. When the *Marie Celeste* did not reply to his signals, Morehouse sent his mate and two seamen to investigate. As they approached the silent, mysterious ship they became increasingly psyched out. Nor did this feeling diminish as they surveyed the deserted deck. Below the mystery deepened.

In the galley the stove was still warm; on the mess table were half-full cups of tea, warm to the touch! Everything else was in normal working order except that there was no crew. The *Marie Celeste*'s seamen had not even bothered to take their pipes or money when they de-

* When the wind vane steered the boat, perfect sail balance was not critically important, so I did not play with it under various sea and wind conditions. Later in the voyage, I did achieve self-steering on any point of sailing, except dead downwind, with the tiller lashed amidship and without using the self-steering gear. This required intimate familiarity with the yacht's performance under all sea and wind conditions. A mere half roll in the mainsail, or one inch in the position of the sheets, would have meant the difference between self-steering success and failure.

parted. The last entry in the log was dated eleven days previously, when the ship was about six miles off the island of Santa Maria in the Azores. So she had sailed herself about 375 miles to where we are right now.

What had happened? There were many guesses; all sounded far-fetched. Then over the years, one after another of the crew turned up, or at least men who claimed to have been aboard when the *Marie Celeste* sailed out of New York harbor. One of these was the cook. He was interviewed by a writer, John Keating, who spent ten years piecing together the story of the *Marie Celeste*, which he finally published in 1930.

Shortly before sailing, the *Marie*'s skipper, Captain Briggs, was still shorthanded, which was not unusual in those days when sailors knew that survival was a better bet under steam than under sail. In a tavern he cried out his tale of woe on the shoulder of a fellow captain, who was also heading for Europe within a few days. This new drinking companion turned out to be more than generous; he could spare three experienced members of his crew at least as far as the Azores when the worst of the crossing would be over. The name of this obliging Good Samaritan? None other than Captain Morehouse of the *Dei Gratia*!

Captain Morehouse must have been a master of improvisation. In an instant he visualized how he could claim salvage on a ship that, if everything went according to plan, would apparently be abandoned while in Bristol condition. Three particularly villainous members of his crew would create general havoc among the crew and officers of the *Marie Celeste* to such an extent that they would abandon their ship voluntarily. Evidently the three *Dei Gratia* fifth columnists were also gourmets. At any rate, they valued the talents of the cook, John Pemberton, so much that they persuaded him to expand their evil triumvirate into an even more evil quartet. And, as it turned out, by the time the Azores hove into sight the crew of the *Marie Celeste* was reduced in number from seventeen to four.

Any time three conspirators deliberately set out to stir up trouble among the confined crew of a ship they are likely to succeed; but they are certain to succeed when the ship's cargo is potable ethyl alcohol. First things first, the three imposters immediately broke out a barrel of alcohol and passed it around the watch off duty. After being drunk for several days it is not surprising that the casualty rate among the crew from falling off yardarms, falling overboard, and so on climbed dramatically.

When land was sighted the mate and the last two of the crew (except for the cook) got into the lifeboat and rowed away from the ship, which they believed, with ample reason, to be damned. This left our four scoundrels, who sailed the *Marie Celeste* to where *Fidelio* is right now.

Then on Friday, December 13, 1872, the *Marie Celeste* and the *Dei Gratia* entered Gibraltar harbor and dropped anchor. Morehouse described to the maritime authorities how he had found the abandoned ship, put a prize crew aboard, and brought her to Gibraltar, which entitled him to a substantial reward for salvage. After protracted hearings the court of inquiry agreed and awarded Captain Morehouse $8,500, one-fifth of the value of the *Marie Ce-*

leste. This is equivalent to about $50,000 in today's currency, so the captain's diabolical plot paid off handsomely, in the short run. As for the long run the record is silent. But I'm sure that the captain eventually reaped all the retribution that he had so sedulously earned.

OCTOBER 29TH: The logbook heading is outlined in red and marked "Red Letter Day." The 3:00 P.M. entry speaks for itself: "Eureka! Glory Hallelujah! I haven't touched the helm since 1:30 P.M., despite the most difficult condition, i.e., a fifteen-foot swell on the quarter, which throws *Fidelio* into a skid, plus variable winds as rain squalls pass over us from time to time."

Don't credit my inventiveness, credit my memory. I finally recalled an article in a yachting magazine. Briefly, the storm jib is acting as a steering sail in the form of a backed staysail set flying from the spinnaker topping lift block, with its foot tied to the samson post. The sheet leads through a block tied to the upper shroud about six feet above the deck level, then via a block tied to the guardrail opposite the tiller and to the tiller itself.

When *Fidelio* heads up too much, increasing pressure on the backed sail puts the tiller up (to windward), and if she falls off too much, a length of shock cord on the leeward side pulls the tiller down. Whatever transpires, this is an immensely satisfying accomplishment. Now I can hope to carry out my original plan of sailing nonstop to Antigua, even with the three days lost experimenting and the seven days lost hove to in gales.

When I wrote "whatever transpires," I must have had a premonition of yet another setback. All afternoon the self-steering sail holds us on course perfectly. Not as precisely as the Hydrovane gear, which would permit us to wander only five degrees on either side of the desired course, but without any attention to the tiller on my part. The self-steering sail might let us wander as much as twenty degrees on either side but averaged out pretty close to the desired course.

My new-found euphoria doesn't last very long. The "red letter day" will end up as black as the nasty squall that blasts over us at 10:00 P.M. The squalls that have come along earlier in the day consisted mainly of rain. I saunter out on deck for my usual check, not expecting any trouble. Suddenly, a screaming blast of wind strikes us. I pull down the mainsail and jib in record time.

But now the new and unfamiliar steering sail arrangement proves my downfall. Its sheet is tied to the tiller, so I rush back and only with difficulty untie it; the wet rope had coagulated like concrete. The halyard is an orange ¼-inch polypropylene line I had rigged through the spinnaker tang block before leaving Shoreham. Now this halyard has also set up like concrete around the main halyard cleat and *under* the main halyard, because there is no other place on the mast to tie it off.

After a futile attempt to untangle it in the dark I rush below to get a torch. All the while the sail is flogging fearfully, in danger of shredding itself to pieces. I am working away at the tangle with my marlinspike when suddenly it gives way under the terrific pressure. The thirty feet of line just disappears with one "whiff" before I can move a finger. The bitter end of this makeshift halyard was tied to a shackle at the foot of the mast and there it parts like a piece of silk thread, and the storm jib blows over the side into the water. Fortunately, the foot of the sail is tied to the samson post so it isn't lost. Thank goodness. This has been my most indispensable sail.

Cursing myself for being such a clumsy fool, I shine the torch on the now-empty block midway between the spreader and the masthead. To put the self-steering sail back in business I will have to climb the mast. Not an easy task even when moored in a calm harbor—a chilling prospect out on the ever-heaving North Atlantic. There is nothing I can do about it until daylight, so I get to work untangling the mess on the foredeck.

11:30 P.M.—Looking at the chart I see that we are close to 36° N. latitude, a parallel that neatly divides Spain from Africa by passing down the center of the Strait of Gibraltar. Just up the Spanish coast where the Guadalquivir River flows into the Atlantic lies the small seaport of Sanlúcar de Barrameda, starting point for many of the great voyages of discovery.

The greatest of these began on September 20, 1519, when Ferdinand Magellan, commanding a fleet of five caravels, embarked on the first circumnavigation of the globe. And the weather when the fleet arrived where we are now was about the same as it is tonight. Over the years the example of courage and fortitude displayed by this lonely, taciturn man has sustained me at times when I was about to throw in the towel.

Christopher Columbus is better known and he was, perhaps, the greatest dead-reckoning navigator of all time. But Magellan's voyage was the longest, the most grueling, the most courageous adventure until the Apollo spacecraft headed for the moon.

Magellan was blessed with the two qualities that make such miraculous achievements possible: courage and faith. Thus, shortly before sailing, this deeply religious man wrote out and signed his last will and testament. He bequeathed most of his estate to various monasteries, including Montserrat, near Barcelona. Fifteen paupers were to be provided with food and clothing, and many bequests were made to religious houses so "that they may pray to God our Lord for my soul." All this before providing for his wife, who was pregnant, and baby son.

Sailing into the harsh southern ocean off Cape Horn where no one had ever sailed before would be trial enough with loyal lieutenants. Magellan's cross came in the form of the captains of his other four ships, who were grandees of Spain and, therefore, were reluctant to take orders from a low-born foreigner. Their leader, Juan de Cartegena, captain of the largest ship in the fleet, first challenged Magellan's leadership shortly after leaving the Canary Islands.

These experienced captains all knew that Magellan's Portuguese countrymen steered southwest when heading for Brazil, so as to pass west of the Cape Verde Islands. In contrast, their admiral inexplicably steered south along the African coast, thereby passing well to the east of the Cape Verde Islands. Nor would the admiral explain why he deviated from the most direct route. This seemed to the Spanish captains to be a gross navigational blunder, and their opinion was vindicated when the fleet was becalmed for twenty stifling hot days in the doldrums.

This ordeal was followed by gales that threatened to overwhelm them. Then, in one thunder squall, the holy fire of Saint Elmo, together with visions of other saints, burned at the masthead so brilliantly that the crew were blinded by their splendor. This heavenly intervention caused the fury of the sea to abate so that the fleet survived intact.

In the incomparable tropical harbor of Rio de Janeiro fresh food was obtained while the sailors, more to the point, enjoyed the favors of the numerous nude brown girls. Doubtless they were reluctant to leave Paradise because they knew that no European had ever sailed south of the Rio de la Plata, which flows into the Atlantic Ocean at the thirty-fifth parallel of south latitude. All the way to 49° south Magellan painstakingly explored every bay, gulf, inlet, and river in the hope of finding the strait that would open the door to the Spice Islands.

At that point, discouraged by the bitter cold weather and sick at heart, he decided to winter in bleak, frigid Port San Julian. Here, inactivity and despair of ever returning home, combined with the Spanish captains' contempt for their admiral, quickly jelled into full-scale mutiny. Three of the admiral's ships joined in the conspiracy to return to Spain. Outwardly, Magellan's situation appeared hopeless. And it would have to anyone else. But, by a daring stratagem, he managed to recapture one of the ships, which so demoralized the remaining mutineers that they meekly capitulated and the admiral was once more in full command.

The three ringleaders were tried and found guilty.*

* Strangely enough, fifty-eight years later at this very spot, Sir Francis Drake, the second man to sail around the world, executed one of his best friends, who was accused of mutinous conduct.

One was beheaded, his body drawn and quartered. When the voyage was resumed in the spring, the other two, including Juan de Cartegena, were left behind in that godforsaken land of giant savages.

It is now 1:00 A.M. I am resting in the cockpit when I see a most unusual sight. A full moon shines behind and through towering squall clouds, at times sparkling on the restless sea. Near the horizon I see a perfect rainbow, not with the colors of the spectrum, but rather a light gray against the black clouds. Is there such a thing as a rainbow (moonbow?) at night? Not that I know of. Yet what I see is a perfect rainbow. A traditional sign of the covenant between God and man.

Death Lurks
in the Night

And doomed to death,
Though fated not to die.
—JOHN DRYDEN

OCTOBER 30TH: Up at the first light of dawn. I now face the arduous task of climbing the mast. I prepare the equipment and lines needed, and I tie a new ⅜-inch terylene line to the bosun's chair; it will serve as the new steering sail halyard. Now follow several abortive attempts to pull myself up the mast.

Even though the sea conditions are about as favorable as can be expected, I don't succeed. When a larger-than-average swell slides under us the boat rolls, perhaps fifteen degrees from vertical. Thus, I wind up spinning around the mast, bumping against it like an amusement park dodg'em car. Bruised and battered, especially on the inside of my thighs, I sit down over a cup of tea to consider the situation. I know that I have no choice; I just have to make it up the mast.

Next, I try hooking the shortest safety line on my harness, sit in the chair and pass it around the mast, hooking the other end to the harness ring. This holds my chest less than a foot from the mast. Then I form a bosun's hitch with the hoisting line over the hook holding the chair. Now I can retain the pitifully small distance gained each time I pull myself up and then rest awhile, surveying the sea and meditating on its vastness.

The best part of an hour passes before I finally reach the spinnaker block and pass the end of the new halyard through it. From here I can see a ship on the horizon that would be invisible from the deck. At least coming down is easier. However, when I reach the deck I lie down trembling and weak as a newborn kitten. One thing I know for certain: These little episodes promote a feeling of humility. Doubtless a young athletic fellow could climb the mast in five or ten minutes. I should have put steps on the mast, but then there are many things I should have done before sailing.

However, I don't feel too bad about my inept efforts to get up the mast. Far better sailors have had even more trouble. Thus, Chichester tried and failed, while Robin Knox-Johnson bungled the job even worse than I did. Then again, the sea conditions may have been more lively when they tried. But Robin's problem was that he left the mainsail up and so could not secure himself to the mast and got buffeted worse than I did. A strange lapse for such an experienced singlehander.

As the sun sets, the squalls, which seem to appear with clocklike regularity each evening, have decided to give us a respite; instead, a steady fifteen-knot breeze caresses our happy ship. As long as these ideal conditions prevail, the steering sail will hold her on course with the precision of an automatic pilot. When I switch on the masthead light, nothing happens; the batteries are flat. (Actually, one battery might be flat, the other partially discharged. I always keep enough juice in one to start the motor.) Rather than charge the batteries I take the easy way out and light the Tilley lamp. I lash it to the hand-rail, where it shines on both the mainsail and the jib. After a cup of cocoa I flop into my bunk for badly needed sleep. It has been an exhausting day, which seems the rule rather than the exception.

At 2:00 A.M. I awaken and notice that the lamp has gone out. I bring it below and am filling it with kerosene when a lurch sends it flying off the table. The last mantle disintegrates. There will be no outside light tonight. I go back to bed (with all my clothes on as usual), hook up the leeboard and doze off, reassured by the fact that we are not very near any of the shipping lanes shown on the chart.

But I can't sleep. Most unusual; usually I can't stay awake. A voice says over and over, "You should charge the batteries right now, turn on the masthead light, and you can still get a couple of hours' sleep."

Tired as I am, some irresistible force makes me get up, start the motor, and clamber up into the cockpit to survey the horizon. Off to port I can see the lights of a ship. After watching it awhile I figure it will cross our path a mile or so ahead of us. I drop down into the cabin to brew some tea. I check the ship's position again a few minutes later. It's closer but I'm not sure of its course. I reach for the big torch, go out on the foredeck, shine it first on the sails then direct it toward the ship. She is still some distance off so I decide to finish my tea.

Three or four minutes later I go forward again and what I see this time stuns me. The ship is only a couple of cables away! We are on a perfect collision course! Unless I do something immediately *Fidelio* will smash into the ship's side in a matter of a minute or two. I rush back to the cockpit, unlash the tiller, put it hard up, and we fall off, missing a collision by about fifty yards. I'm in a state of shock, as row after row of bright lights slide past. If I had remained in my bunk it would have been the end, because I hadn't touched the tiller, sheets, or self-steering sail even once since sunset. I send up a prayer of gratitude to whoever out there urged me to get up.

As this voyage progresses, the more devoutly I believe in the power of mind/spirit to guide and govern our lives throughout each day. I repeat and meditate on Breviary entries such as "My guardian angel surrounds and protects me at all times." If we are sincere and fervent someone in the spirit world will watch over us. If we don't believe this we will lack such protection. "Coincidence" is a word that should be eliminated from the English language.

OCTOBER 31ST: Things look more cheerful on this last day of October, which was a first day in other ways. The first day the temperature reached seventy degrees in the cabin. The first day without squalls. The first day without some sort of problem or emergency. The first day of ideal sailing conditions, all day soft warm air and a sparkling blue sea. For the first time I change jibs without oilies on and without getting wet.

I lie out in the sunshine for a while, then come to a momentous decision. For the first time since leaving Shoreham I am going to bathe, trim my beard and mustache, and even put on clean clothes. Already the problems, gales, and near disasters of the past few weeks are being replaced in my imagination by the warm trade winds that are calling to us from just below the southern horizon.

NOVEMBER 1ST: The new month starts auspiciously as *Fidelio* crosses the thirty-fifth parallel of north latitude, and so we are at last south of the area of frequent gales. About time, too. The jury-rigged self-steering works so well that I decide to press on nonstop to the West Indies.

We are now in the same latitude as Cádiz and Seville, where most of the Spanish galleons set sail for the New World. While living in Spain I visited the maritime museum in Palma de Majorca, where there is an old Spanish chart of the North Atlantic that plots the routes of all these early voyages. Most outbound ships called at the Canary Islands for refreshment, but many cut the corner and bypassed the islands, perhaps to avoid hostile squadrons reported to be cruising near them. The latter route is the one I plan to follow. When nearing the West Indies on their way to Santo Domingo, they usually passed between the islands of Dominica and Martinique or through the

Guadeloupe Channel. I expect to follow in their wake through the latter passage.

The RDF set, which has been wet and therefore silent, is drying out in the sun. It suddenly comes to life. Madeira comes in loud and clear, bearing 150°, exactly where it should be. The windless weather is most unusual, the pilot assures me; the Portuguese trade winds seldom fail. If only we could motor out of the vacuum.

Actually, while I worry about lack of progress, I enjoy these periods of calm when the transparent depths disclose the creatures beneath us. The electric blue-green dorados are still with us, but only eight now instead of nine. I've seen lots of large, brown sea turtles, usually escorted by striped pilot fish. As far as I can tell, they (like me) are always alone. Two fat little fish also stay with us, carefully keeping in the shadow of the boat. They are curious and investigate everything I throw overboard.

At 11:00 P.M. a breeze finally arrives from the southeast! Unheard of. According to the wind rose on the chart the chances of this happening are nil. Out of nine hundred reports from this five-degree square of ocean, not one mariner had encountered a southeast wind. Perhaps I should write and tell the Admiralty that such things do occur. As a matter of fact, for three straight days the wind blows from this unorthodox quadrant. This means we are sailing close-hauled, which is usually no fun.

NOVEMBER 3RD: Dawn. This must be what the fourth dimension of space/time feels like. A magical, enchanted fairyland; silent, misty, transparent clouds nearby and on the horizon denser clouds in rows like courtiers awaiting the arrival of their king (the sun) in a properly reverential stance.

I am gazing at these cloud towers hovering over the endless, empty ocean when the water is magically replaced by an equally endless lawn of clouds, crowded with millions of my fellow men and women, all of whom are gazing at me intently. I'm no longer on *Fidelio*. Instead, I'm standing naked in a witness-box and they are staring at my nakedness with apparent loathing. Those millions of eyes overwhelm me with shuddering humility, which, I suddenly know, is what opens the doors to Paradise; when I admit that the evil I see in others is really in me.

Why do I weep? Because of this shattering humility? Or because I now know with absolute certainty that heaven and hell are one and the same.

Am I awakening from a nightmare? Or a vision of Paradise? Whichever, I realize that there can be no progress along the path to enlightenment until one feels utterly crushed and annihilated; wholly dependent on God's mercy and providence. Salvation comes from *knowing* that I am nothing, God is all.

10:00 A.M.—Really eerie—oily, flat calm, empty horizon sharp as a knife edge. Meditating as the sun rose encouraged a spiritual mood that lasted too long. I should be working on the engine, which seems the only way out of this apparently extensive area of calm.

4:00 P.M.—The mystery of the engine is solved. I accidentally dropped a screwdriver down into the bilge and was groping around for it when I came upon half of one of the engine bolts that sheared off. The nut and locknut were still on the threaded end. It had sheared off below the level of the engine bed. I see no possible way of repairing it without lifting the engine out, then digging out and replacing the other half of the bolt that is still embedded in the concrete. A major job, which I certainly can't do at sea.

Fidelio, fortunately, will steer herself to windward for hours at a time without attention, so I have plenty of time to relax and listen to the radio. A BBC-accented voice informs me that Israel plans to honor ex-President Truman with a special monument or memorial of some sort. Israel? Why Israel? I can't think of any logical reason. This reminds me of the early days of the Truman Administration, when I was a young scientist working on the Manhattan Project.

Three weeks before the first atomic bombs were dropped on Japan, we knew that the test in New Mexico had succeeded. Most of us hoped that the bomb would be dropped on a small Japanese town only after first warning the Japanese government to evacuate the people. Instead, the bombs were dropped without warning on Hiroshima and Nagasaki, killing 120,000 persons instantaneously, with thousands more destined to suffer lingering deaths from radiation sickness or burns.

Since Japan had made peace overtures and was ready to collapse anyway, this mass murder of civilians was unnecessary from a military standpoint. Never mind that! We young idealists hoped that the horror of Hiroshima and Nagasaki would have favorable repercussions in the long run. Wouldn't it be made clear to even the most empty-headed politicians and generals that their hallowed concepts of war, balance of power, and all the rest were now obsolete?

By no means, as subsequent events ranging from Korea to Vietnam proved. In our innocence we failed to allow for the final frailty of mankind: the love of wielding power, and that power corrupts. Truman really had no choice when confronted with the atomic bomb decision. He had suddenly become the most powerful man in the world. But power cannot be wielded benevolently, or with compassion. Hence, Truman's arrogant, inhuman boast that he did not lose even five minutes' sleep over the fate of those fellow human beings who were exterminated and crippled at his command. What was he doing at the time? Playing the piano?

NOVEMBER 6TH: Another milestone. We have dropped below thirty degrees north latitude. This is the latitude of Jacksonville, Florida. In North American distances, we have sailed from Nova Scotia to Miami. Only enough tobacco remains for one more pipe, which will be savored for the final time after dinner tonight. Well, I have managed very well without the other vices.

Four weeks alone at sea. It's an experience that makes me acutely aware of the mortality of all life and, hence, to quote Dr. Johnson, "It wonderfully concentrates the mind." Or, at least, I see things differently. For example, tonight I have been reading Homer and, for the first time, I identify with the people as well as the story. I have always viewed the Greek religion and all their gods as a sort of childish joke. How could these intelligent, reasonable people believe in the divinity of all those gods with all of their human failings? Yet, we know that the

Greeks, at least those of the Homeric era, did believe in them, and they were certainly at least as enlightened as we are.

These ancients "saw" and talked to their gods constantly. What exactly took place? Did they see what the Spanish soldiers saw when Santiago, on his white charger, led them into battle? What Joan of Arc saw when the saints spoke to her from a cloud of light? What Ramakrishna saw when he assured the person he was talking to that God was much more real than that person? Did the image of the god appear in their mind's eye? Did God appear in the form of celestial light?

In whatever form the Greek gods manifested themselves, there can be no doubt about the powerful part they played in the lives of their devotees. Thus, the Greek who felt deserted by the god with whom he had a personal relationship felt truly abandoned and hopeless. And with good reason. Homer explains the demise of more than one powerful warrior: "Whoever rejects the goddess [Athene] and relies only on his own strength will fail miserably through that same divine power."

So we should not be surprised by the important position held by the gods in the world of Homer. Every thought, every action reflects the influence of the divine presence. I can only conclude—contrary to what I previously believed—that the Greeks were a god-intoxicated people, to an extent only equaled in the Western world by a handful of mystics. No society has ever deferred to the divine with such loyalty and reverence. Shortly before his death, Hector's mind is at ease because the outcome is in the hands of the gods. He philosophically tells his wife,

"No Greek will kill me, unless Heaven permits him; and what mortal can evade his destiny?"

NOVEMBER 7TH: When I climbed into the cockpit this morning I had company, the first flying fish of the voyage. It is about six inches long with three reddish-brown bands horizontally crossing its belly.

As the night stealthily envelops us, it brings with it the most spectacular display of phosphorescence that I have yet seen—as if thousands of sparklers are flaming in the water on either side, while behind us trails a fiery wake ten to fifteen feet long. The fireworks are caused by plankton, tiny sea animals, which light up when disturbed. Sometimes the sea water glows when I pump it into the sink.

NOVEMBER 8TH: 2:00 A.M.—The sea and wind have gradually built up until the self-steering sail can no longer cope, so I steer for a while. Soon I cannot cope. Or rather, to continue would invite trouble. The seas are huge and, from time to time, one of them throws the bow into the wind enough to spill the wind out of the jib; it then refills with a sound like thunder, threatening to dismast us or rip the sail. As usual we heave to with the storm jib sheeted flat. This drill, familiar though it is by now, takes the best part of an hour, during which I wonder if I'm on a boat or a bucking bronco.

4:00 A.M.—I am out on deck scanning the horizon for ships. Suddenly the storm jib starts flapping in the wind as if it wasn't hanked on to the forestays, like a flag rippling out from its pole. My God in Heaven! The jib is hanked on the stay okay, but the stay is shackled to the end of the turnbuckle, which has worked loose from its barrel. In short, the mast is completely unsupported from the bow. If this had occurred two hours earlier, *Fidelio* would have lost her mast.

I release the sheets and the halyards. Then, as the forestay swings past, I grab it and rescrew the threaded end into its barrel. However, I shall wait until morning to adjust the tension of the stays prior to getting underway. Shaken but relieved, I drop below to brew a cup of tea. Whatever caused me to drop the sails and heave to at that particular moment? I offer up one more prayer of thanksgiving to whoever is watching over us. After all, being dismasted is about the worst thing that can happen to a sailboat—other than sinking—especially when you can't use the motor.

This close call is due to carelessness on my part. All the shroud turnbuckles are open-barrel bronze. When the tension on the shrouds is right, you bend a cotter pin through and around the threads, which prevent it from unscrewing. The stay turnbuckles are closed-barrel stainless steel with no provision for preventing unscrewing. I forgot to check them and will do so every day from now on.

NOVEMBER 9TH: A quiet, calm night at last. *Fidelio* sails along on course while I get some much-needed sleep. It's getting warmer and I'm drinking more of my dwindling supply of water. Heaving that ten gallons overboard may have helped at a time of emergency, but what now? The Canary Islands and the Cape Verde Islands are about the same distance from where we are right now. Going to the former would mean backtracking against the trades, a prospect that does not appeal to me even though I have detailed charts of them. Going to the latter would pose no problem since we are headed for them right now and it wouldn't be much out of the way. Yet I don't have any charts or sailing directions for them. A situation to be avoided by a singlehander if at all possible.

At least this is the way I rationalize my decision to carry on across the Atlantic without stopping. After all, I should be able to catch rainwater or distill sea water. Or, as a last resort, I can drink sea water. Bombard proved conclusively that this is safe, providing a person is not already dehydrated when he starts.

At 1:30 A.M. I am reefing the mainsail when I see a brilliant white trail of light in the eastern sky, which ends in an explosive flash, a meteor that, heated white hot, probably disintegrated. Several are visible every night but nothing like this one.

NOVEMBER 10TH: 8:00 A.M.—log 1,874 sea miles. We are well within the limits of the northeast trades, and if this is typical I'm not going to like them, wind variable and sea rough! Was up about ten times last night; I thought we had broached to or something had broken, but everything intact. Now I envy Father Boylan, who only gets up twice in the night.

Noon position: 21° 19′ W., 23° 51′ N.

Just as I finish these calculations, a wave comes from nowhere, sweeps over the boat, and cascades twenty to thirty gallons of water down through the companionway hatch. Water now stands on my bunk. The instrument panel is dripping, as are the emergency flares above my bunk. Even my favorite Renoir reproduction gets soaked for the first time

PART II

Across the Atlantic

Boisterous
Trade Winds

Look! The enlightened person is conscious neither of time past nor of time to come but only of the eternal present moment.
— MEISTER ECKHART

NOVEMBER 12TH: The trade wind continues to blow at Force 7, judging by the twelve- to fourteen-foot waves. According to the chart the wind never attains this force in this area. So am I overestimating the height of the waves? There is no doubt that people in small boats tend to exaggerate the height of large waves, probably by one-third or more. But when it comes to small waves I think my method measures them more accurately. When I stand on the second step of the companionway ladder, I am exactly 3½ feet above the surface of the sea in which we are floating. This means my eye level is nine feet above the water.

The critical factor in measuring waves is to do so only when your platform is level. So, when we are in a trough, I watch the waves with one eye, the inclinometer with the other. Right now the crest of the average wave is three to five feet above eye level.

Strangely enough, although conditions are moderate, the motion is as bad as any I have experienced. Could it be due to the erratic course produced by the self-steering sail, which can barely cope with these conditions? From time to time it goes aback and then fills; the sudden pull on the tiller seems more than enough to break either it or the rudder. I decide to replace the ⅜-inch line leading to the tiller with ¼-inch line and hope that it will break before the tiller or rudder.

Once again the cabin becomes a shambles with water everywhere. I can't even sit down to eat but remain standing, strapped in front of the stove. Nothing stays on the table for even a second; the fiddles may as well not be there. Spillage becomes a serious problem because I can't afford to waste anything. Yet pouring from the teakettle into a mug often results in the loss of half a mug of water. But I have been heaving to at night since the trade wind got so boisterous and I can't also heave to in the daytime just to avoid some discomfort.

As evening approaches, I decide to steer all night and make up some lost time. Usually I leave the steering sail in charge all night, but under these conditions it needs help from time to time, so I couldn't get any sleep anyway. To fortify myself, I prepare a large pot of vegetable soup and tie it on the stove. Soon a delicious aroma fills the cabin. To stir it I have to release the shock cord holding it in place. I say to myself, "Don't let this spill," when a big lurch comes along. Instead of trying to catch myself, I try to catch the soup. My head smashes against the ledge under the window with stunning force, splitting open a gash on my cheekbone, like a watermelon being dropped on concrete. It makes me sick and dizzy, especially when I contemplate the soup-spattered cabin. After treating the cut I go on deck, drop the sails, and heave to, then clean up the mess. So this is trade-wind sailing! Dinner turns out to be crackers and a can of cold chili.

NOVEMBER 13TH: Dawn brings a change in breeze from fresh to gentle and a sea change from rough to smooth. Now I welcome the chance to relax and meditate!

After meditating on today's office in the Breviary, I cook my usual breakfast of oatmeal and finish up with a mug of tea out in the cockpit. I notice a lone dolphin: where are all the others?

For the past couple of days a number of dolphins have been cavorting all around us. Probably a school that has scattered while chasing flying fish. Some of them kept *Fidelio* company, although they don't ride the bow wave, which is a dolphin trademark; *Fidelio* is just too slow to make this tactic feasible. They are about six feet in length, brownish backs, whitish bellies, with rings around their eyes; they remind me of an old-time comedian whose name I can't recall. Instead of wearing real spectacles, he painted them around his eyes. After watching them I conclude that no other animal approaches the beauty and graceful perfection of dolphins.

There is no sign of the school this morning except for this laggard who swims lazily back and forth close behind us. I go below and come back with a can of sardines. When I drop one into the water the dolphin noses it, turns away, then reluctantly decides to eat it, mimicking a person who doesn't want to hurt another person's feelings.

An hour passes; lying on my stomach over the transom, I proffer the last sardine, which I hold in my hand just above the water. The dolphin accepts it in such a dainty fashion, without touching my fingers, that I conclude that I am consorting with a female. Perhaps a divorcée seeking male companionship? Seriously, a lone dolphin might be either ill or old and therefore unable to keep up with the school. But my dolphin's teeth look young while her eyes look not only healthy but joyful and mischievous.

I decide to name her Christabel after the heroine in Coleridge's poem.

I can plainly feel empathy emanating from Christabel, feelings of love and compassion for me. I feel this very strongly. One look at those expressive eyes and the most hardened skeptic would feel it too. I wonder if she receives the same empathy from me that I certainly feel for her?

I talk to her and tell her about *Fidelio* and the storms we have weathered, that I am going to turn west today, cross the Atlantic and that I would very much like her to keep me company. She answers with a series of squeaky whistles, then dives off to the side a hundred feet or so, explodes out of the water in a leap that carries her well above the wave tops. This is obviously her way of responding to my attentions.

The tremendous emotional impact of this encounter

surprises me. If instead I had met another yacht, I would welcome her crew with friendly feelings, but there would be an unacknowledged barrier between us that obstructs most human relationships. It's well and good to say that human love should be unconditional and nonexclusive, but it rarely is. In contrast, there are no barriers between man and dolphin. Or, on a different level, between man and dog. And this has been true as far back as ancient Greece. Since that time we have heard of dolphins rescuing drowning sailors and swimmers, of dolphins guiding ships away from dangerous reefs and piloting them into safe harbors.

Man's inhumane treatment of dolphins has been on a par with man's inhumane treatment of all other animals and also of his own kind. Japanese fishermen systematically murder thousands of dolphins each year. Our tuna fleet did the same until a law was passed that reduced the slaughter to some extent. Historically, fishermen have always viewed dolphins as competitive enemies who deserved to be ruthlessly exterminated.

In view of this record it is an astonishing fact that a dolphin has never been known to attack a human being. This is not because dolphins lack the killer instinct. In fact, dolphins are accomplished shark killers. Their technique: ramming the shark in a vulnerable area with their beaks. Why do dolphins distinguish between sharks and humans? Because they recognize Homo sapiens as their brothers and sisters?

3:00 P.M.—Christabel has me almost hypnotized. Or rather, I feel a sense of well-being, a high akin to that of the state of superconsciousness. I float away into the astral realm of dolphins. Might not they have their history, poetry, music—about which we know nothing?

4:00 P.M.—Christabel seems restless and excited. Is she trying to tell me something? I sense she is saying goodbye to me.

Sure enough, she heads east toward Africa, swooping in graceful arcs in and out of the sea. In the distance I can see the school and among them I imagine her friends and relatives. For the first time I feel alone and desolate.

By 6:00 P.M. we are nearing the twentieth parallel, so I gybe. We have turned the corner at last, heading west across the Atlantic, near the point at which many of the galleons had turned west after leaving Spain some 440 years before *Fidelio*'s passage. At this moment we are about two hundred miles north of the Cape Verde Islands and about four hundred miles off the coast of Africa. The distance to Antigua is about 2,350 sea miles. We turn west thirty-five days after leaving England.

The slow going has depressed me, but in this respect I have had many illustrious predecessors. One, for example, was the clipper ship *Duke of Sutherland* on which the twenty-year-old Joseph Conrad shipped as an ordinary seaman. She left England on October 15, 1878, and sighted the Cape Verde Islands thirty-eight days later, after being held up by fierce westerly gales in the Bay of Biscay. Think of that. *Fidelio* and a clipper ship neck to neck after thirty-five days. The *Duke* must have encountered even more gales and calms than *Fidelio* did.

Any wind-driven ship requires favorable winds to reach her destination. When the weather gods don't cooperate the results can be catastrophic, as in the case of the German barkentine *Tiger*. She, too, sailed down the English Channel en route to New York. She encountered head winds or no wind at all the entire way. After 124 days and while still two hundred miles off Cape Hatteras, the starving crew were finally rescued by the British steamship *Nebo*.

On April 1, 1791, Captain George Vancouver sailed from Falmouth in the 99-foot *Discovery* on his way to the northwest coast of North America, which he charted for the first time. The *Discovery* reached the Canary Islands on April 29. It is some comfort to know that *Fidelio* reached the latitude of the Canaries in exactly the same time, twenty-eight days.

All day I've been thinking about the second entry in today's office: "The world at its best isn't miserable, isn't hateful, it is mad. The pursuit of worldly pleasures and ambitions as ends in themselves is madness, because it disregards the real purpose of life, which is to know God in ourselves and in other people. To be sane is to be aware of this truth."

Is that to say "normal" people are insane? A more charitable phrase might be "out of touch with reality." The two cold warriors have some fifty thousand nuclear warheads in their arsenals. When and if they are ever fired they represent "mutually assured destruction" (MAD). The President and the Pentagon tell us that the more weapons we have the less chance that they will ever be used. Anyone who can say this may not be legally insane but certainly exists in a peculiar dream world.

NOVEMBER 14TH: This is trade-wind sailing as I had

always imagined it would be. Warm soothing wind, too gentle now, deep blue sea, tropical sunshine. I sit on the cabin leaning back against the dinghy, entranced by the procession of puffball clouds overhead and the schools of flying fish ricocheting off one wave after another. *Fidelio* seems to be sailing across the boundary of the two worlds: the finite and infinite.

A key to self-realization is not to worry about the future or think about the past. But I can't seem to help worrying about some projections I have just made. Namely, it is becoming increasingly apparent that I am going to run out of both food and water before reaching land.

The lunch menu: crackers, sardines, sauerkraut, and rice pudding for dessert. However, I will not enjoy this kind of lunch again, for the empty sauerkraut and rice-pudding cans now sinking to the bottom of the ocean were the last of their kind on board.

The wind gradually diminishes during the afternoon and my high spirits since turning west fade away with it. A misty smog or dust envelops us, which I imagine is blowing from the Sahara Desert. I seem to feel a malevolent presence on and all around *Fidelio*.

Up to now I have only been conscious of a positive, helpful presence—my "guardian angel" or the old sea captain who piloted *Fidelio* through the Bay of Biscay gale. Yet, in this world and within each person, evil, at least the potential for it, is certainly as tangible as good. And more so in those unseen "other worlds" that become all too real to the lone sailor surrounded by an endless sea.

As the sun sets a partial explanation for the oppressive atmosphere is revealed. I write in the log book:

"Brilliant, continuous flashes of light to the east of us. Encompassing an arc of twenty to thirty degrees on or below the horizon. No sound; in fact, deathly silence. It's eerie, weird. An hour of it and I'm still baffled, uneasy. Could it be naval gunfire? Heat lightning? With no reports or thunder? With no visible clouds? Stars are now clearly visible just above the horizon."

The right side of my brain takes over. At any rate, I vividly sense the presence of evil, tormented entities. Are they "ghosts" from one of the most horrifying episodes in the history of the sea?

This event transpired a long distance behind us in time, but only a short distance from us in sea miles. In fact, if I felt like climbing the mast—heaven forbid—I might be able to catch a glimpse of Cape Blanc, the southwestern tip of Spanish Morocco, or, at least, see the offshore reefs where this macabre event unfolded.

In June 1816, the French frigate *Medusa* sailed from the naval base at Rochefort headed for the West African colony of Senegal. Jammed aboard were some four hundred souls ranging from the families of hopeful colonists to a contingent of soldiers. Leading the expedition was Hugues de Chaumareys, a favorite of the newly installed king, Louis XVIII. This vain dandy was undoubtedly the most incompetent man ever to be given command of a ship.

Thus, after rounding Cape Finisterre, the *Medusa* followed closely the course of *Fidelio* until reaching 20° north latitude, where she bore off to the southeast (*Fidelio* turned due west). Shortly after turning and with the weather perfect, Captain de Chaumareys ran his ship hard aground on the uncharted and ever-shifting Arguin Bank, which extends some fifty miles off the coast of Africa.

The *Medusa* was a strongly built ship and in no danger of breaking up in even the heaviest weather. Nevertheless, in a panic, the captain, most of the crew and a few favored families took to the lifeboats. About 167 of the less fortunate passengers and soldiers were left to fend for themselves on a ship that, presumably, might sink at any moment. Under the direction of a carpenter they hastily built a raft using the ship's topmasts and spars. When finished the raft barely floated. Should they stay with the ship or gamble on the raft?

Seventeen crew members were sufficiently knowledgeable (or drunk) to stay with the ship. The remainder of the passengers opted for the raft, a gamble that only fifteen of them survived. And several of these survivors never recovered either mentally or physically from their frightful ordeal.

With 150 people in a space measuring about twenty feet by sixty feet, there wasn't room to sit or lie down. Moreover, when the last of the castaways climbed on the raft, the hapless occupants were standing in water up to their waists. With no lifelines of any kind, simply to stay on the raft required the utmost concentration.

After only two days under a broiling sun, with no food, little water and no sleep, their nerves began to unravel. The reason is one all of us have experienced—the feeling of claustrophobia after only a few minutes on a crowded elevator. Imagine if that elevator were half filled with water! No wonder insanity and hysteria replaced plain old fear. As fate ordained, most of the men were armed: crew members with knives, soldiers with sabers and muskets, gentlemen with swords.

The center of the raft, which was relatively stable and safe, was occupied mainly by army officers and soldiers. At either end of the raft were civilians, crew members, and lower ranking soldiers. Suddenly a shouting tide of madmen armed with knives attacked the officers in the center, who slashed back with their heavy sabers. Those who fell seriously wounded were thrown into the sea; after all, the unacknowledged objective of the fighting was to create more room on the raft. The bloody slaughter continued, off and on, all night.

By morning the population on the raft had been reduced to sixty. Half of these were wounded and clearly could not survive for long. Compelling hunger soon led to a solution to the food problem. Each day the officer in charge selected one among those who seemed about to die; the victim was then executed and eaten.

In this way fifteen men managed to survive. They were found, blackened by the sun and half dead, by a search party from the town of St. Louis, in Senegal, some 250 miles down the coast from the stranded *Medusa* and the aimlessly drifting raft.

Later on, needless to say, the French nation was appalled by these acts of cannibalism and even more appalled when the naval court-martial sentenced Captain de Chaumareys to a prison term of only three years for abandoning his ship and passengers.

Mind over Matter

The physicist does not discover, he creates his universe.
—HENRY MARGENAU

Anyone who is not shocked by quantum theory has not understood it.
—NIELS BOHR

If the statistical predictions of quantum theory are true, an objective universe cannot exist apart from our senses and consciousness.
—H. S. STAPP (paraphrased)

NOVEMBER 15TH: Light winds all night so I leave the genoa up. I'm standing looking out of the companionway just as the rim of the sun appears. A great opportunity to check the accuracy of the compass against the sun's amplitude. So I take bearings and then, following the procedure described in *Reed's,* I calculate the west variation at eleven degrees, which means (if I did it all correctly) the compass is accurate to within one degree.

3:00 P.M.—I retract all my complaints about trade-wind sailing. A fantastic day. Sea slight, wind Force 2, warm sunshine, deep blue sky, porpoises chasing flying fish, beauty everywhere.

After five weeks of solitude I have finally managed to root out ingrained practical values. I have jettisoned them over the side to the bottom of the Atlantic. It is revealed to me with absolute certainty that I survived the various close encounters with death not due to "luck" or "coincidence" but rather due to the concentrated power of my own mind. Or the intervention of my guardian angel. Does it matter which? They are the same thing. My guardian angel (or God) exists "out there" as well as within me (and you).

The background for this revelation was prepared during the long winter nights in London, when I pored over the lives of the mystics, which, strangely enough, led me to explore the "new physics."

The average person doesn't believe that mind/spirit can control or alter the physical world, although we see this phenomenon in action every day. For example, we know that stress and negative emotions can make us physically sick while we irrationally doubt that positive emotions and thoughts can cure our illnesses or prevent them from occurring in the first place.

This skepticism seems to be much more prevalent in the materialistic West than in the more spiritually oriented East or in "primitive" societies, where the ability to perform spectacular examples of the power of mind over matter is taken for granted. To illustrate, yogis in India and Tibet can control their bodies to an unbelievable degree. With sufficient training, adepts can virtually suspend bodily functions for long periods of time. Many have chosen to be buried for hours and even days with only their training to keep them alive; when released, they are perfectly normal. Yet the doctors of medicine assure us that the brain is irreparably damaged if deprived of normal amounts of oxygen for more than a few minutes.

Other yogis can warm or cool their bodies at will. Just reading about the initiation ceremonies of one sect will cool you when it's 110° in the shade! On a winter's night when the temperature has plunged to zero or below, the aspirants hike to a frozen lake, cut a hole in the ice, and sit naked around it. An attendant (clothed?) dips a sheet in the icy water, then drapes it around the aspirant's body. As soon as the heat of his body has dried the sheet, the process is repeated. This goes on all night. The newly ordained yogi who has dried the most sheets attains the highest status in the community.

How can knowledgeable, fully-clothed Americans believe such a story when they become chilly if their living-room temperature dips two or three degrees below 68° F? One way is to read Alexandra David-Neel's book, *Magic and Mystery in Tibet*. She lived in Tibet for fourteen years. A chapter in her book describes the art of *tumo*, or warming oneself. She tells us:

"Only those who are qualified to undertake the training may hope to enjoy its fruit. The most important qualifications are: To be already skilled in the various breathing techniques; and to be capable of a perfect concentration of mind, going as far as the trance in which thoughts become visualized. The process always combines prolonged retention of the breath and visualization of fire."

My own experience confirms that *tumo* can, indeed, be mastered, at least to a limited degree, even by the untrained westerner. For example, the only heat in my room in the London house was a coin-operated gas heater in the fireplace. You put in a shilling and the heater went on for about ten minutes. This obviously was an expensive way to keep warm.

At first I froze in that room during December and January when the English sun sets at about 3:30 P.M. and the temperature often sinks to below 30° F. The key to mastering *tumo* is one-pointed mind concentration, which can be achieved only when you are completely relaxed. Breathing exercises help you relax, so night after night I practiced controlled breathing, followed by excluding all thoughts from my mind but one; namely, I visualized a blazing log fire in the fireplace. When I started this program I wore a sweater plus my heavy down jacket. The room temperature was in the low fifties. Eventually, at the same room temperature I was comfortable wearing only a bathrobe of medium weight and warmth.

In other parts of the world a much warmer ordeal known as fire-walking is practiced. Some years ago the *National Geographic* magazine covered such a ceremony in Sri Lanka. It is held annually to honor a Hindu god. The devotees spend three months preparing for the event during which they devote every waking hour to meditation, prayer, and communion with their god. Each participant knows that if he diligently follows this routine he will please the god to such an extent that the god will enable him to walk with impunity over the red-hot coals. In some years all participants walk safely through the fire. In other years participants whose faith or mind concentration is not sufficiently one-pointed have suffered major burns and even death.

On the evening of the final day a pit twenty feet long and six feet wide was filled with seasoned hardwood logs, which had burned down to red-hot (1,320° F) embers by 4:00 A.M. when the twenty fire-walkers were ready to perform. The twenty included boys and girls as well as men and women. All crossed the twenty feet of coals safely and with no sign of burns. Some crossed the pit several times. One young man scooped up a handful of burning embers and dropped them on his shoulders. When asked how he did it, one man replied, "Faith, total faith in my gods."

Similar fire-walking ceremonies occur in many other countries, and the literature on the phenomenon is quite extensive. I discussed fire-walking with a friend who embraces the common-sense outlook of most Americans. His reaction: "They probably wore specially made asbestos shoes and garments." He was nonplussed when I showed him the *Geographic* color photographs which clearly revealed that the fire-walkers were barefoot and wore garments of what appeared to be ordinary cotton cloth. Nevertheless, he still felt that some sort of trick was involved.

But, *how were* they able to walk through fire without even scorching their garments, let alone their bare feet? Did their god perform a miracle? Or did one-pointed mind concentration make their bodies impervious to fire?

Or are we talking about the same thing? Here we must go beyond the definitions and semantics so dear to rational common-sense thought. When we attempt to define the word "God," we fall into a quagmire from which it is difficult to escape.

John begins his gospel: "In the beginning was the word, and the word was with God; and *the word was God*" (emphasis added). This is profoundly true; our reality is a function of the word—our language. We are programmed by the reality created by our language and our society to believe that fire will burn us and that cancer will kill us. Our problem is to create a new reality for ourselves, wherein fire will not burn us and cancer will not kill us. I now see how the new physics can combine with age-old mysticism to show us how to create this new reality, which, obviously, is capable of transforming our lives.

THE NEW PHYSICS

My own belief is that the mind controls and affects matter only when it is in tune with and strengthened by that mighty supernatural force that keeps the universe going from one heartbeat to the next.* What you choose to call

---

* Jung defined this force as the collective unconscious of the human race and cited "the well-known fact that anyone who has found access to the unconscious, involuntarily exercises an influence on his environment. The deepening and broadening of his consciousness produces the kind of effect that the primitives call 'mana.' "(Webster defines mana as "the impersonal, supernatural force to which certain primitive peoples attribute good fortune, magical powers, etc.") Jung believed further that we will remain forever imprisoned in our three-dimensional, sense-bound reality until we are able to

this force is immaterial. To define is to limit, and certainly the mysterious power running the universe must be omnipotent to an unlimited degree.

Is human mind/spirit a manifestation of this power? If so, this explains why mind/spirit creates and controls matter rather than vice versa. When I use the word "supernatural" I do not intend to contrast the power of the mind with that of an exterior supernatural power. The two are identical. To make such a distinction is to embrace dualism, the source of all error and illusion.

This conclusion is not based on mystical theology but rather on recent developments in theoretical and subatomic physics, although, of course, the mystics have been telling us the same thing for at least 2,500 years. Namely, to transcend three-dimensional reality a person must discriminate between what is real and eternal versus what is illusionary and transitory. Such discrimination always leads to one conclusion: Mind/spirit is real and eternal, while the material world is an illusion.

Why does our society find this so difficult to believe? Because it violates what we call "common sense." The material world is all too real. Moreover, the vast majority of people know for sure that *they* can't create or control matter. Or can they, without being aware of this ability? As William Blake said, "If the sun began to doubt, it would immediately go out." Doubters are operating on the wavelength of common sense, which is the reality perceived by the five senses.

---

replace our dominating, suffocating intellect with humble one-pointed faith in the unconscious powers that exist within us.

But according to Buckminster Fuller (and the new physics) this reality constitutes only a tiny fraction (say one percent) of the reality all around us and "out there." The other ninety-nine percent is beyond the comprehension of the five senses. Thus, we see and hear only a tiny fraction of what could be seen and heard if our eyes and ears had a wider, more sensitive range. To transcend the five senses, reliance on "common sense" or reasoning power must be abandoned. This is why Einstein defined common sense as "the prejudices frozen into our minds before the age of eighteen."

Most people are doubters because they cling to the reality they can see and touch, and reject any other. Just as, in 1930, the world's most renowned astronomer proved conclusively that man could never travel in space. And for thousands of years a majority of mankind believed that the sun circled the earth; their senses were deceiving them, just as *our senses often deceive us.*

The "new physics" is a term used to differentiate it from Newtonian physics, on which all scientific laws were based until the early years of this century when the quantum* and relativity theories of Max Planck and Albert Einstein demolished forever our mechanical way of inter-

---

* Max Planck discovered that the energy of heat radiation (and light) was not emitted continuously, but rather in the form of separate and distinct units or packets of energy. Einstein dubbed these units of energy "quanta," thereby naming the quantum theory. In the final analysis there are no smallest particles of matter; there are only these packets of energy or quanta. Our universe is composed of them, and this explains the overriding importance of the quantum theory and why it is the basis of all aspects of life on earth.

preting the physical world. They revealed that Newton's laws of motion only work in the three-dimensional reality comprehended by the five senses.

Newton's three laws accurately describe and define mechanics here on earth and, when combined with the rule of inverse squares, they also accurately describe and define the orbits of the planets. However, they do so for the wrong reasons. Newton fit the solution to the problem.

He assumed that a planet was attracted to the sun (and kept in orbit) by a force varying directly as the product of their masses and inversely as the square of the distance between them. From this he further assumed that every particle of matter in the universe attracts every other particle in accordance with this formula. Moreover, this gravitational force operates instantaneously over limitless distances.

The problem is that gravity cannot be a constant attraction between two masses, a force that works without any time lapse. Einstein had conclusively proven that no physical force could act faster than the speed of light, which meant that gravity was something other than Newton's force of attraction between two masses.

Newton assumed that space was "flat," so that all the axioms of plane geometry could be applied in space. Actually, there are *not* any straight lines in space, the sum of the angles of a triangle do *not* equal 180°, and so on. Nor are Newton's laws one hundred percent correct here on earth. However, the margin of error is, for most purposes, too small to matter. This is why Newton's laws are still

·taught in school, even after Einstein showed them to be inaccurate.

The problem of how and why the planets and other heavenly bodies move could not be solved until Einstein published his general theory of relativity. The answer, of course, is that space is curved. The mass of the sun curves the space around it. The planets move in an elliptical orbit because this is the path that requires the least distance and time in curved space-time.

For three hundred years Newton's mechanical laws have been accepted as gospel truth and applied in many areas with unfortunate results. One example is their application to the human body. Until quite recently medical science has viewed the human body as a machine, with the machine controlling the mind rather than vice versa. This fostered the belief that only doctors can cure us, and the result has been a mushrooming of doctors and hospitals. Happily, today more and more doctors are using biofeedback and other techniques based on the mind's ability to cure the body.

My doctor (this was before I stopped going to doctors), who was no believer in the power of mind over body, nevertheless told me that he thought that ninety percent of his patients could have cured themselves of their complaints. The person whose mind is in control of all aspects of his life will also be in control of his health. If this control weakens and illness occurs, concentrating the mind on the problem while excluding all else will trigger the immune system to fight the invading disease.

When the new physics says that mind creates and

sustains matter, this is literally and continuously true at the subatomic level. Matter is being continuously created and dissolved by energy, i.e., a particle is energy one instant, what the human senses perceive to be matter the next. On the human level we refer to "mind/spirit," on the subatomic level to energy. They are the same thing.

Physicists have carried out countless laboratory experiments which have demonstrated that mind does, indeed, affect matter. They reveal, for example, that the observer influences the event being observed. Moreover, the more one-pointed the concentration of the observer, the greater the influence on the event being observed.

Perhaps the most mind-boggling product of the physics revolution is Bell's Theorem, which some physicists consider to be the most revolutionary discovery in the history of mankind. It postulates that if the quantum and relativity theories are, in fact, valid (numerous tests and experiments have, without exception, proven them to be true), then an "objective universe" (i.e., one apart from our consciousness) cannot exist. That is, the world "out there" is an illusion constructed by the mind, based on the five senses. Or, more accurately, it is not an illusion to the human senses and consciousness; it is an illusion in terms of a higher reality, in terms of higher space/time dimensions.

That is to say, the table I'm writing on seems solid because my senses are deceiving me. The same holds for the oceans, mountains, in fact the entire earth. All are 99.99 percent empty space. (Actually, they are one hundred percent empty space because there is no such thing as "solid" matter.) And this is the way they all may appear to beings, entities, or spirits who exist in different universes or dimensions of space, time, and consciousness. Or, instead of empty space, in their fourth- or fifth-dimension realities, they may see constructs quite different from my table or the oceans and mountains. The residents of these other worlds coexist with ours and are all around us. A handful of humans are in touch with these other worlds and identify them collectively as the "spirit world."

NOVEMBER 16TH: 3:00 A.M.—The weather can change in a hurry. Squalls all around but none have hit us yet. The net result is variable winds, which means I am changing from one tack to the other too often. It seems like this is all I do because it takes me about forty-five minutes in the dark to rerig the steering sail and its lines to the tiller, the preventer, the sheets, and so on.

8:00 A.M.—Showers from time to time. In these light airs the steering sail needs constant adjustment to keep the sails filled.

6:00 P.M.—Dinner. Am I having spaghetti more and more often because the choices are becoming fewer and fewer? An unbelievable sunset lifts my consciousness to superconscious heights.

The Whales

God is telling us every minute of every day what actions and what thoughts are best for us. Some people call this infallible inner voice "God's Will," others call it conscience.

*

To experience samadhi *(cosmic consciousness) or the vision and union with God, the devotee must be constantly recollected and outside the world of duality. All things must automatically be accepted without any excitement or disquietude of mind.*

—R. W. B.

NOVEMBER 17TH: Scanning the horizon astern, I am thrilled to see a sail off to starboard which, with the aid of binoculars, resolves itself into twin running sails. What if it's Jeff and Ron, friends who left before I did but were going to spend some time in the Canaries? They had rigged twins. Unlikely, but whoever it is they might very well intercept me for a "gam." After all, seeing another yacht in this part of the Atlantic is an event. I go below and trim my beard and mustache just in case. However, two hours later they are still a couple of miles behind us, now off to port. They must be heading for Trinidad. Probably they never saw *Fidelio* because the twins effectively block any view ahead.

Strangely enough, I am relieved at not having to face my fellow men at this particular time. To do so would break the spell, the vision and more acute awareness of the precious gift of life, both human and animal. For three days, two more graceful shearwaters have been soaring back and forth across our wake, courteously investigating the scraps I throw for them. I feel their friendship for me and I'm sure they feel mine for them.

NOVEMBER 19TH: It's 3:00 A.M.. At sea bad things happen with alarm-clock punctuality at 3:00 A.M. I change jibs to better cope with a wind-filled squall. I am clutching the sailbag with one hand, transferring my safety line with the other, when I slip on the deck and go sprawling down into the cockpit, peeling off about eight inches of skin. I have a painfully bruised and bloody shin, but am thankful not to have suffered a worse injury. At least I am not as preoccupied now with my own welfare as I had been earlier in the voyage. Past regrets and future fears are being crowded out of an eternal Now, by the eternal sea unchanged in a million or more years.

Later on, as I change the bandage on my shin (it tends to soak up moisture from the salty sea air) a major decision arises; how to serve my last tin of hamburgers? In chili? In a thick soup? I knew all along I would fry them with potatoes and onions, also the last. What a treat!

Now it is 10:00 P.M. A crescent moon softly lights a magical tropic night. If the gentle breeze persists maybe I can get a few hours of uninterrupted sleep. Well, three hours beats one or two. At 1:00 A.M. a squall rouses me out of a deep sleep and I find the mainsail about to blow out. I wriggle into harness and go out and reef it.

NOVEMBER 20TH: A dead calm today. Which makes me acutely aware that I should start rationing food. Instead, I'm gobbling down everything good that is left. Just now the last can of grapefruit and the last peanuts. Only a few staples left.

I gaze down through the transparent water and realize that I have seen no signs of pollution at all. Yet, Thor Heyerdahl, on the Ra expedition, and others in whose track I am following described the pollution as acute, especially from congealed oil. I have seen none. Maybe the ecology effort is proving effective. It may be due, in part, to the severe penalties for discharging oil, which are printed right on the Admiralty chart of the North Atlantic.

At 3:00 P.M. a pod of whales, majestic and slow moving, circle around us spouting water about ten feet into the air when they surface to breathe. There must be many dozens in the pod because I can see several surfacing at any one time. The large ones are about forty feet in length—perhaps even longer, because all I can see of them is part of their backs and fins. One crosses our bow only a few feet away and I nervously remember all the yachts that have been struck and sunk by whales. They, however, completely ignore *Fidelio* and her red bottom. They keep us company for an hour, leave, and then show up again at 7:00 P.M.

It occurs to me that today marks my fortieth day alone at sea. I realize from my experience during these days the profound truth of Buddha's doctrine that the source of human misery and suffering is desire. Only by conquering desire can we achieve peace of mind.

I'm sure I've been as attached to money, sex, liquor, gambling, tobacco—you name it—as the most unregenerate of my fellows. But remove temptation, and the worldly environment that enthrones these pleasures, and what do we have? An absence of desire. For days I have not thought once about any of these, except when I saw the other yacht, which immediately triggered visions of a drink and a smoke. Which suggests that none of these things, no matter how attached we are to them, is satisfying in itself, or an end in itself.

But how are we to attain a state of nondesire amid the distractions and temptations of everyday living in the world? After all, not many people have the opportunity to spend forty days alone. First, we must understand the psychology of these desires which are the source of our unhappiness. Suppose that the object of our desire is a cigarette. We may try to buy a pack, or bum one. Failing that, we restlessly think about one. When we finally get one and inhale the smoke our mind is at rest. Due to the tobacco? No. It's just that so long as the mind is restless it cannot be at peace. But when it is inactive (asleep) we find peace and serenity, because there are no longer thoughts of some desired object. So it is not the object that gives us peace and contentment but rather the absence of thought. What we really and truly desire is the absence of desire, not this or that object or pleasure.

This is why mind/spirit has no desires at all, nor any likes or dislikes. Desire and aversion, likes and dislikes are the exclusive function of the physical body. Once mind/spirit gains control of the body, the desire for trivialities, which is the cause of restlessness, discontent, unhappiness and misery, can easily be mastered.

NOVEMBER 21ST: Becalmed again! This is all I need. To me no wind means no food and no water for the final few days of the voyage.

I'm meditating on one passage in today's office: "Grace and inspiration are given when and to the extent to which a person gives up self-will and abandons himself moment-by-moment, through constant recollectedness and nonattachment, to the will of God."

In other words, we must learn to believe implicitly that everything that happens to us moment by moment, hour by hour, and day by day is designed to bring us to our final end for which we were born: to know the infinite bliss of divine union.

This doctrine, which is the foundation of all who have climbed the spiritual heights, was beautifully explained by a French Jesuit, Jean Pierre de Caussade (1675–1751), in the spiritual classic *Self-Abandonment to Divine Providence,* published after his death. In it he repeatedly stresses the importance of "the sacrament of the present moment. . . ." Namely, "fidelity to God's plan in the loving acceptance of all that God sends us at every moment.

"If man fulfills his part, God will do the rest. Grace will take full control of him, and the wonders that it will work in him surpass all man's understanding." Man's part of this mysterious equation "consists merely in accepting what most frequently cannot be avoided, and in suffering with love, that is to say, with resignation and sweetness, what is too often endured with weariness and discontent.

"Do not ask me what is the secret of finding this treasure. There is no secret. This treasure is everywhere. It is offered to us at every moment and in every place.

"If we are able to envisage each moment as the manifestation of the will of God, we shall find in it all that our heart can desire. When the event of the moment terrifies, starves, strips, and attacks all the senses, it is just at that moment that it nourishes, enriches, and vitalizes faith, which laughs at (and is freed by) the losses of the senses.

"It is the secret method of divine wisdom to impoverish the senses while enriching the heart, so that the latter is filled in proportion to the painful emptiness that the former experience."

What a superhuman doctrine! Take heart, Rodger! If before this voyage ends I suffer from hunger and thirst what does that matter? It will nourish, enrich, and vitalize my soul if the doctrine of de Caussade is right. And an inner voice tells me that he is right and that this truth is all-important.

NOVEMBER 22ND: In the logbook I note that the solitude must be getting to me, or it was a month ago. Now I'm certain that Jack Kennedy and Aldous Huxley died on November 22, not October 22.

Now several interrelated problems begin to dominate my thinking. There is no longer any doubt; I will run out of food and water before reaching Antigua at the present rate of progress, which promises to become slower rather than faster, since the bottom is becoming more and more foul. We are now sporting a bumper crop of barnacles and grass that are very difficult to remove.

The shortage of water is my own fault. Doubtless I would have survived if I hadn't jettisoned those ten gallons in the gale off Finisterre. As for food, my appetite has been greater than usual, stimulated by the sudden deprivation of both alcohol and tobacco. This was especially true in the cold northern latitudes, although I wasn't aware of it at the time. If so, why have I lost weight? In addition, quite a bit of food has been spoiled by sea water seeping into supposedly watertight plastic containers.

There are a lot of Wilson's or maybe British storm petrels (known to sailors as Mother Carey's chickens) around here. This tiny sea bird (seven inches long), which appears to walk up and down the waves, is easy to identify. Black body, broad white band on the back behind the wings, long legs ending in yellow webbed feet.

The pictures in my bird book of the two species look exactly alike to me but there the similarity ends. Their breeding and summer ranges are a world apart. These fairylike storm birds subsist on plankton, though they often follow ships for the marine life churned up by the propeller or fishing boats for the tiny scraps left by gulls and other large birds.

How did the name Mother Carey's chickens originate? There is more than one explanation. The most common is derived from the legend of the sea witch Mother Carey, who is custodian of Davy Jones's locker, the home of those who drown at sea. She sends her chickens to monitor ships in distress. If the ship sinks and the crew perishes, the souls of good sailors who pray for deliverance are saved. But the souls of wicked sailors, pirates, mutineers, and the like are sentenced by Mother Carey to inhabit forever the bodies of her chickens, doomed to wander without rest from sea to endless sea. Well, watching these free, graceful birds, I can quickly think of many worse fates.

In my opinion, a more likely explanation is that the name derives from *Mater Cara* or Beloved Mother, i.e., Our Lady, the Virgin Mary. The appearance of the water-walking petrels beside a ship before or during a gale is a sign that the Queen of Heaven will guide them safely through it. One of these explanations must be wrong.

The British storm petrel breeds during the northern summer along the west coast of Ireland, Scotland, and the wild, windswept islands to the north. In the fall they head south to the waters off South Africa, where the cold, north-flowing Benguela current meets the warm, powerful Agulhas current, which flows southward along the East African coast. The result is surface water rich in the plankton that attracts petrels by the millions. This yearly migration adds up to a round trip of some 20,000 miles.

The Wilson's storm petrels travel even farther. They breed in Antarctica and nearby islands, then migrate as far north as Labrador and Greenland. This represents a round trip of at least 25,000 miles. Moreover, they breed under the most severe conditions. For example, even though they breed in the Antarctic summer their burrows are often buried by snow or falling ice, making it impossible for the parents to feed their offspring.

Petrels mate for life, but after the fledglings are on their own the parents leave the burrow separately on their way north and apparently do not see one another until the next breeding season. At that time the male arrives a few days before the female in order to prepare the burrow by lining it with moss and penguin feathers. The mates return each year to the same burrow! How do they find it after an ocean voyage of 12,500 miles? No one knows for sure.

The two shearwaters that have been following us are giants compared to the petrels. Their stiff wings, which must span between four and five feet, remind me of the wings of a glider.

I call out to them, "You had better make a left turn soon if you hope to reach Tristan da Cunha in time to breed." At that remote island in the South Atlantic (where a few Wilson's petrels also breed) shearwaters occupy burrows and tunnels which they line with grass. They spend the northern summer in the western North Atlantic. When autumn approaches they cross the Atlantic, then near the coast of Northern Europe turn south until they reach their island home.

Last of the Food

Father, I have no one else to blame. Alas, I sink in the well these very hands have dug. —ANONYMOUS

NOVEMBER 24TH: The weather continues to vary from glassy calms to Force-1 or -2 zephyrs. Such light airs prove more exhausting than when there is plenty of wind. Not only is the heat enervating; so is the constant gybing, raising, and lowering sails in an effort to capitalize on every catspaw. When I see the rippling wind patterns approaching, I quickly hoist the sails and stand on the lee rail to help them fill. Minutes later the breathless calm returns, the sails flog in the sizable swell, the visiting card from storms farther north.

I sum up my feelings in the log: "This is not funny.

I'm going to run out of food and water even if the trade winds resume their normal force. If the calm persists, if *Fidelio* should be dismasted, lose her rudder, or otherwise be immobilized, I'm in real trouble. This is an unfrequented part of the Atlantic Ocean and one could drift here for months without seeing a ship." I soon have more reason to worry. Today's noon-to-noon run adds up to a morale-destroying total of three miles. Where is the west-flowing current? Evidently it responds to the wind like a pilot fish to a turtle.

One obvious solution to the food problem is to catch fish. Unfortunately, among the things I forgot to bring are fish hooks. So I get busy and start bending and filing some eyebolt rings into what I hope will serve as fish hooks. As for water, I expect to catch rainwater and also distill sea water. However, to be on the safe side I start to ration fresh water by drinking two mugs of sea water a day.

A large black-and-gold butterfly floats and dips around us. Where did it come from? The nearest land is the Cape Verde Islands, about 975 miles behind us.

The only thing I have seen since being becalmed is the butterfly, no birds and no fish. The crystal-clear water beneath reveals nothing. How far down can I see? I drop the lead line over the side and watch it sink. When it reaches the end at one hundred feet I can still see it plainly.

I know I should take advantage of the calm to go over the side and scrape off some of the barnacles and salad; both are growing luxuriously on our bottom. However, an almost paralyzing apathy grips me, whether from my monotonous diet or lack of stimulating company I can't tell. Nothing seems to matter, and I prefer to simply sit and meditate or write down my thoughts.

As evening approaches I don't even bother to cook. I prefer to be nourished by an incredibly flamboyant sunset offset by the full moon rising amid rose-tinted, fleecy clouds, which are hastening toward the setting sun. Evidently the trade wind is still blowing higher up. There is no comparison at all between sunsets on land versus these at sea.

I can sense the presence of the One who walked with Evelyn Underhill along the Western road leading away from the town in which she grew up. I memorized some of the lines of a poem she wrote about that experience.

> The Western road goes streaming out to seek the
>   cleanly wild.
> It pours the cities' dim desires towards the undefiled.
> It sweeps between the huddled homes about its
>   eddies grown,
> To fill the space between the city and the sown.
> The torrents of that seething tide who is there that
>   can see?
> There's One who walked with starry feet the Western
>   road by me.
>
> Behold He lent me as we went the vision of a seer,
> Behold I saw the life of men, the life of God shine
>   clear.
> I saw the hidden spirit's thrust; I saw the race fulfill
> The spiral of its steep ascent predestined of the will.

Yet not unled, but shepherded by one they may not
   see,
The One who walked with starry feet the Western
   road by me.

Evelyn Underhill was an otherwise ordinary English
lady who wrote an extraordinary book about mysticism,
which was published in 1911. Her central theme parallels,
of course, that of the mystics of every time and place.
However, she presents the ever-recurring conflict between
the spiritual and the material life in a refreshingly original
manner. Her main points as I recall them can be sum-
marized as follows:

Why accept as our standard a world of material
values whose existence is affirmed by nothing more trust-
worthy than the sense impressions of "normal" men and
woman, those imperfect and easily deceived channels of
communication?

Materialism is a fruit of the intellect that creates its
own problems and then makes itself miserable trying to
solve them. As a result, the ability to think and reason
now becomes the enemy that enslaves us and from which
we must escape if we are to gain freedom and the resulting
inner serenity it produces. In short, materialism can, and
must, be replaced with something better. That "something" proves elusive because, until we gain that freedom,
our traditional speech and social mores encourage us to
conceal rather than to reveal and share with one another
the unique and lovely world in which we live.

This explains, in part, why sanity consists in sharing
the hallucinations of our neighbors.

We see a sham world because we lead a sham life. We do not know ourselves; hence, we do not understand the true nature of our senses and instincts, and so attribute wrong value to their suggestions and declarations concerning our relation to the external world. That world, which we have distorted by identifying it with our own self-regarding arrangements of its elements, has got to reassume for us the character of Ultimate Reality, of God.

Ultimate Reality is an independent spiritual world, existing on other and higher levels of consciousness, unconditioned by the apparent world of sense. To know it and live in it is man's true destiny. But how? By paying careful attention to the news available to all who wish to receive it, of a world of Absolute Beauty, Absolute Truth, and Absolute Life, beyond the realm of time and space.

Many of us try to translate this news (and inevitably distort it in the process) into the language of beauty, which is simple Reality seen with the eyes of love.

To enter this divine world, we must first break with the sense world, which blocks the birth and development of the spiritual consciousness; which, in turn, leads to ever closer and deeper dependence on and appropriation of the fullness of the Divine Life—that is, a conscious participation in an active union with the infinite and eternal.

To accomplish this transition requires the cultivation of disinterested love, which is difficult, if not impossible, so long as our outlook is conditioned by the exclusive action of the will to live. Disinterested love thrives on a diet of detachment, i.e., the death of preferences of all kinds, even those that seem to other people the very proofs of virtue. The mountain peak of detachment (or holy indifference) can only be reached via the steep slope labeled "self-mortification."

The object of self-mortification, like the object of all purgation, is freedom—freedom from the bondage of the senses, the bondage of desire, the bondage of human relationships, and the bondage of ambition. A point is finally reached when the ups and downs of mortal life are accepted with true indifference and no longer trouble the soul.

This state will be scorned as "escapism" by existentially troubled people. And this is as good a word as any to label what Evelyn Underhill is talking about. Saint John of the Cross says the same thing, although there is no word in Spanish equivalent to "escapism." "Oh, how well it is that the soul should withdraw from all things, flee from business and live in boundless tranquillity, lest anything however small, or the slightest turmoil should disturb or turn away the bosom of the Beloved."

To summarize: Evelyn Underhill is telling us exactly what the new physics has been telling us since 1964, when Bell's revolutionary theorem forever changed our way of viewing the universe. Bell's Theorem ended the reign of the law of duality and enthroned in its place the law of unity.

NOVEMBER 26TH: 3:00 A.M.—Gybe for about the tenth time today (now yesterday). The trade wind breeze is fickle when it's here at all. I need sleep but not as urgently as I need to go faster.

9:00 A.M.—Log 3,250 sea miles. The light variable breeze has died out and the sails barely fill, then empty with a bang, as the swells sweep majestically by.

NOVEMBER 27TH: Finally got around to doing some long overdue house-cleaning chores. Cleaned the sink, stove, and surroundings, which were still a mess dating back to the Bay of Biscay gales. Very little wind but rough due to a big confused swell.

In contrast to the crystal-clear air of recent days a ghostly mist or dust envelops *Fidelio* and the ocean. No birds or flying fish since this period of calm began. Could this be dust from a storm in the Sahara Desert? Driven by gale winds which created the swell? I estimate the swells average about one and one half city blocks in length and about twenty feet from trough to peak. Superimposed on the swell are waves that account for the rocky motion.

NOVEMBER 28TH: At 1:00 A.M., the fiftieth day alone at sea, the trade wind returns in full force. So much so that I get up at 3:00 A.M. when waves begin to break over us, filling the cockpit and splashing down into the cabin through the open companionway hatch.

I am once again working strapped in at the stove when I need something in the cupboard under it. To open it I must release the strap. Just as I do this, a lurch sends me reeling backward. My spine hits the edge of the table with terrific force. I can actually feel the dent in it (my spine, not the table). Fortunately, this blow doesn't seem to activate the backache problem.

The steering sail cannot cope adequately with the strong, gusty wind. As result, it steers the yacht in an S-shaped course instead of a straight line. This, of course, slows us down appreciably. Despite this handicap and our barnacle-covered bottom, the day's run turns out to be ninety-two miles under the heavily reefed main and the small jib, which gives some idea of the strength of the trade winds at this stage of the voyage. The log reads 4,025 sea miles from Shoreham.

NOVEMBER 30TH: Breakfast was a real feast by my rapidly deteriorating standards; the last of the oatmeal and the last of the brown sugar. *Nothing is left* but spaghetti. Not a pleasant prospect, as much as I like spaghetti.

Where is the rest of the world? Since leaving England, I haven't seen a single airplane.

1:00 A.M.—The sky looks like a witch's caldron. I can plainly see the squall clouds writhing in the moonlight, gathering together their strength to harass poor *Fidelio*. So this is how the squalls are born? I reluctantly go out and reduce sail.

3:00 A.M.—The squalls have roared away and I should get more sail up, but my legs feel as though they were made of jelly. I'm going to bed. So I starve before reaching land.

DECEMBER 1ST: The first day of December brings a welcome respite. A windless day, squalls all around, but not near, with their progeny; magnificent rainbows.

With only two gallons of fresh water left, the time has come to manufacture some. First, I place the one-burner primus under the companionway stairs, fill an old teakettle with sea water. To its spout I fit one end of a fifteen-foot length of five-eighths inch plastic tubing with the other end bending out into the cockpit and into a one-gallon jug. I tightly wrap wet towels around the tubing and place a five-gallon jerry can filled with sea water on the cabin top with a one-quarter inch tube siphoning out of it down onto the towel-wrapped distillation tubing.

Soon steam is rising from the kettle, condensing and falling drop by drop into the jug. But, at the end of two hours, I have collected less than one mug of fresh water. I calculate that for each pint of fresh water obtained, about three pints of paraffin would be consumed and the crude apparatus would require my constant attention for the entire day. How can I improve its efficiency?

In contrast to the slowness of the distillation process, when the next squall comes along, I hastily spread a tarp over the cockpit and, though we were only on the edge of it, collect a pint of brackish water in only a few minutes. Obviously, in the center of one of these deluges I could get plenty of water. However, even though squalls are all around, I never seem to be at the center, which ordinarily would please me. Between squalls the ominously silent calms continue to oppress the atmosphere.

I search through the lockers hoping to come across some overlooked delicacy. Unfortunately, there is nothing left but spaghetti. I like spaghetti and brought plenty just in case of such an emergency as this. But this diet quickly becomes monotonous and probably inadequate. At any rate, when the trade wind returns at full strength, I seem to be suffering more than ever from lethargy. I write in the log: "Conditions seem to be getting wilder and rougher; or am I getting weaker and weaker? Omitted breakfast today. Spaghetti twice a day is enough. Even I can't take it three times a day."

Surrounded by lovely rainbows but no rain falling on

Fidelio. Not enough wind to steer toward the squalls producing the rainbows in the hope of catching a few raindrops.

Here it is December. If only I could get word to Kathy, who must be worried by now. I told her I should reach Antigua in about forty-five days and no more than sixty! Well at the rate I'm going it will be a lot more than sixty, if I get there at all! Maybe it is just as well I can't, on the theory that no news is good news.

Spaghetti hour and still calm. Bombard in this same area and time of year experienced twenty windless days. He wrote, "In the area of the West Indies, in November and December, there are two days of wind for every ten days of flat calm." A gross exaggeration, of course, but I know how he felt. I should drop the sails, which flog as we rock back and forth, but the light-weight genoa occasionally fills enough to keep some steerage anyway.

10:00 P.M.—Still no wind.

DECEMBER 2ND: The sunrise today brings a vision of paradise. The eastern sky is a bouquet of Renoir flowers, pale yellow to reddish violet. But still no wind. I'm running out of shopping days until Christmas. Progress; a miserable fifteen miles in twenty-four hours. Since the sails have not been hoisted even once this means the west-flowing current is back in business. At this rate I will never reach land by Christmas, at least not alive. Squalls all around and calms between them. Just as in the doldrums. Perhaps the jet stream has gotten off course and deflected the trade winds farther south, or farther north? I bet on south and decide to steer a more southerly course when the wind returns.

Before I get any weaker I know I should get to work on the bottom. I unlash the dinghy and wrestle it over the side, get in with my scraper, and get to work. After half an hour of work I have cleaned about four square feet. There is a carpet of marine growth about one-quarter to one-half inch thick that resembles a clipped lawn, and it adheres like cement, as do the barnacles.

Then I notice a king-sized squall approaching. I scramble back on deck as it hits us. Lots of wind and lightning, but no thunder. Strange, By now it's too late to resume the bottom work so I haul the dinghy back on board, using the main halyard and winch for muscle, jockey it back in place, and lash it down. I'm ravenously hungry even for spaghetti, which I eat out on the foredeck contemplating another glorious sunset. Then the sunset turns into sheer magic. *Fidelio* glides silently between and toward towering black clouds, like a lone rider through Monument Valley.

DECEMBER 3RD: The towering black clouds have given way to puffballs, which should herald the winds' return later in the morning.

Noon position: 48° 00′ west longitude which compares to 61° 40′ for Antigua, which translates into nine hundred land miles, which seem unattainable when you have little water, little food, and no wind. Then when I go out on deck I see cat's-paws dancing toward us from the east.

6:00 P.M.—At last we are flying along at a good six knots. With a water-line length of twenty-seven feet, *Fidelio* should have a top speed of seven knots but in practice it's only six. The prop slows her by, perhaps, half a knot and the heavy ferrocement hull also slows her. The claim that ferrocement hulls can be made that are lighter than wood and as light as fiberglass simply isn't true, at least not in the case of *Fidelio*.

Reluctantly, I start boiling sea water for spaghetti.

DECEMBER 4TH: The wind has finally returned to its usual Force 6 to 7 and, despite the turbulent seas, from time to time I can see an ever-circling platoon of dorados flash past. This encourages me to finish work on the fish hook and soon I have it needle sharp, hook shaped with a barb. For bait, since no flying fish have come aboard recently, I wrap some spaghetti sauce in a small, folded piece of cloth and sew it tightly shut, bury the hook in it and trail it overboard with a weight on the line. My friends pay no attention to it at all.

All day and until the charmed hour of 3:00 A.M. we smash through the twelve- to fifteen-foot seas with only the steering sail and deep-reefed mainsail set. I can doze for only a few minutes at a time. However, I'm asleep when a squall hits at 3:00 A.M. The black storm clouds are etched against the horizon by the waning moon, an example of "wind before rain," I think, just as cold, driving rain envelops us.

I grope my way forward still in my bedroom slippers and what greets me is bad news. The steering sail has vanished! Then I see it dragging in the water. I also see the snatch block, which had been shackled to the spinnaker tang, lying on the deck. It had sheared off at the jaw, yet it should have withstood twenty times the force exerted by the little storm jib. Probably metal fatigue.

I can do nothing about it until daylight, so I pull the

storm jib aboard, drop the mainsail, and go wearily back to bed. But I can't get to sleep. I still have about eight hundred miles to go. At our present rate of progress it might take from eight to ten or twelve days to make it. Without the self-steering sail it could take twice as long. I am going to run out of both food and water within a few days. This means I must climb the mast again to replace the broken block. Only this time I am much weaker.

DECEMBER 5TH: At dawn I am out rigging the bosun's chair. Although the motion is fairly violent I try to pull myself up. I'm too weak. I give up until the sea calms somewhat and spend the morning trying to get the yacht to self-steer with two jibs hoisted on a single forestay. This effort not only ends in failure as before, but results in another serious setback.

I want to switch the headsails so I drop them, release a spinnaker pole, and lay it across the deck without securing it while I release the other pole. *Fidelio* heels and before I can grab it, the spinnaker pole slides over the side and disappears forever. To make up for this carelessness I am determined to get up the mast and replace the broken block. My mind will give me the needed strength.

1:00 P.M.—For lunch an extra large plate of spaghetti for extra strength. When I finish it, I wonder if I'm not adding more weight than strength. Well, it's too late now.

Once again I climb into the bosun's chair, pass the short safety line around the mast and hook it back into the harness ring. This prevents me from banging against the mast too much when I get up higher. Next, take up the slack in the hoisting line. Now I pull up with all my strength and rise maybe eight inches or a foot; secure the gain with the bosun's hitch, lean back against my harness, and rest.

After an hour of this I've climbed about twelve feet or half the distance to the spinnaker block. I'm even weaker than I thought and have to rest longer after each effort. Realistically, I know I will never make it since I'm about to faint from fatigue and overexertion. I also know that I must make it up there.

So I unhook the bosun's hitch and pull as hard as I can—and up I go! Five or six feet! Someone on deck must have pulled on the dangling end of the hoisting line! I'm sure of it, I could feel it in the line. I look down. I can't *see* anyone but I *know* someone is there!

I admit I'm so tired that I'm half asleep. Maybe I'm dreaming, I don't know. In any event, I had better take advantage of whoever is there before I wake up.

Once again I pull on the hoisting line and presto— I'm up to the spinnaker block! I call out in a loud voice to whomever may have helped me: "Thank you, Mr. Mariner, thank you guardian angels one and all."

Then, feeling foolish, I sit there in a daze for a while thinking about what has happened. To me it's a miracle. Yet until this voyage no one could have been more skeptical regarding psychokinetic phenomena, such as *tumo* and fire-walking. Now I'm a believer. It's as simple as that. I will no longer argue with someone who views what has just happened as an example of assistance rendered by unseen entities who are "out there" as well as all around us.

Now that I'm up here I'm painfully aware of a lot

more cuts and bruises, plus a strained back and groin from slamming into the mast and probably due to overexertion in my weakened condition. When I am about to shackle on the block, I drop the pliers, which bounce off the deck into the Atlantic. I'm ready to give up when I notice that the pin has a hole in it so that I am able to tighten it with my marlinespike. When I come down I lie on the deck for half a hour before I'm strong enough to get under way. Even then it takes twice as long as usual. The spaghetti diet isn't providing sufficient protein to give me strength. Another whole day wasted.

During the night we sail through the New York to South America shipping lane without even showing a light. Nor do I look out even once. It would just require too much effort. My back is so bad that to get out of my bunk I have to lift my left leg with both hands out and down onto the floor. So when the usual squalls hit, I stay put and hope for the best. With only the steering sail and reefed main, *Fidelio* can carry on through all but the very worst squalls.

DECEMBER 6TH: 10:00 A.M.—Now I need to gybe and this is a hassle because the portside blocks for the self-steering lines are stolen from the bosun's chair tackle and I was too exhausted yesterday to replace them.

Noon—King-sized squalls are all around us, so I decide to try and capture some rain. Rig a tarp across the cockpit and wait, and wait, and wait. Rain, rain all around but only a few drops here.

1:00 P.M.—Sails back up, which is becoming a major chore due to various aches and pains.

Now I'm worried about the rudder. During the past thousand miles the gudgeons have become looser and looser. The self-steering sail exerts continuous and sometimes dangerously great pressure on the tiller and rudder.

2:30 P.M.—Noon position: 51° 00′ W. 17° 30′ N.

The Sargasso Sea

Alone, alone, all, all alone,
Alone on a wide, wide sea!
And never a saint took pity on
My soul in agony.
                    —COLERIDGE,

DECEMBER 7TH: This is one of those halcyon days I envisioned while in the cold stormy north; a perfect Force-3 breeze, ideal for the genoa. But as desperately as I need to go faster, I know that to wrestle it out and hoist it would completely deplete my small reserve of strength, which I am conserving for the next emergency. There is another reason to linger in this area. We are nearing the South America–North Africa shipping lane and, while this does not sound as if it would be jammed with traffic, the longer we are near it the greater the chance of intercepting a ship. As we jog along I ponder an important decision about the dinner menu: whether to have McCormick or Knorr sauce on the spaghetti. I decide on the McCormick and it tastes great.

I've been meditating over tomorrow's office, which includes one of my favorite passages:

> The will is free and we are at liberty to identify our being either exclusively with our selfness and its interests (in which case we shall be either passively damned or actively fiendish), or exclusively with the divine within us and without (in which case we shall be saints).

Why does this priceless sentence remind me of Valerie and Jean and their husbands, the two Johns? Because the words "passively damned" and "actively fiendish" perfectly describe the consequences of the aimless, accidental lives led by these two couples. I should know. After all, I lived with Valerie and Jean for over a year while I was building *Fidelio*.

Their lives were so improbable that I eventually hope to translate their story into a novel. Like most people, these two couples drifted from one accident to another instead of planning and controlling their lives. To illustrate, the men ran off with other women, then returned and were temporarily reconciled. The wives attempted suicide. The husbands smuggled drugs, landed in jail in Morocco, and so it went. Why? Because each partner—at least this was true of the men—loved themselves more than their spouses, God, or their neighbor.

Why were these outwardly attractive, normal-appearing people "either passively damned or actively fiendish"? There are two kinds of love, human and divine. The former is preoccupied with "self-interest," the latter, "exclusively with the divine within us and without."

Human love is exclusive and conditional, whereas divine love is nonexclusive and unconditional. The former is fallible and always fails us in time. The latter is infallible and never fails us.

Divine love—loving the divine—must be the perfect spiritual support precisely because the divine is unseen and abstract rather than material. God is not subject to the decay and imperfection that, sooner or later, defeats mortal man. In this connection, are not neurosis and anxiety the result of anticipating the arrival of this decay and imperfection? Only God, Spirit, Immortal Soul can triumph over death.

Certainly another human being cannot supply this answer to the riddle of life as we all know to our sorrow. He or she, as a finite, fallible being, cannot long postpone deterioration and extinction; whereas, we yearn for something transcendental and eternal. It can be found only by renouncing the transitory world and waking up to the truth that once the goal of divine union becomes our only goal, at that moment we join the immortals. The alternative is to continue to lead the same old meaningless, accidental lives.

4:00 A.M.—I'm drinking a mug of my "iced" tea, sitting in the cockpit, when I see a flag ahead of us sticking up from what appear to be several plastic buoys. I head for it and catch it with the boathook. I haul in the floats and part of a fishing net. The net contains a luxurious growth of yellow seaweed.

This could only come from the Sargasso Sea, which is just to the north of us. This vast stagnant expanse of seaweed is confined by clockwise currents that prevent it from escaping. Where is the fishing boat that owned this net? Another mystery of the sea?

I scoop up a pail of weed-filled water, pour it out on deck, and marvel at the miraculously camouflaged life revealed. Tiny fish seem to have the exact patterns of the Sargasso weeds painted on them. There are other tiny wriggling creatures that I do not recognize, in fact, can hardly see at all. Perhaps they are infant eels? The long migrations of these snakelike fish add up to one of the chief glories and mysteries of nature.

The adult eels set up housekeeping in the estuaries and tidal rivers of eastern North America and western Europe. When the time to spawn approaches, the eels embark on the long journey to the Sargasso Sea, where the female deposits her eggs in the depths. When the baby eels hatch they ascend to the surface, seeking the anonymity of life among the weeds. Those that survive the various predators live and grow in size and strength among the slowly drifting patches of weed.

When the eels are nearing maturity, they embark upon an incredible journey of their own. They retrace the route followed by their elders until they reach the home territory of their ancestors. Without exception the new generation whose parents came from an American river or lagoon return to that very same spot, as do the offspring of

European parents. How is this possible? How do they know where to go? To attribute this phenomenon to "instinct" simply begs the question.

How then can we explain it? We know that the eels hatch thousands of miles from their ancestral waters, alone in the hostile vastness of the sea. The traveler has no advance knowledge of ocean and tidal currents that may deflect their course, nor of the ocean floor as it shoals toward the land. The eels, after all, have not previously been where they are now going. How then do they do it? No one knows.

The Sargasso Sea has always fascinated me ever since I saw a movie about it some forty years ago. The movie was called *The Sea of Missing Ships.* Hundreds of derelict ships had drifted into the Sargasso Sea, some with crews and passengers still aboard. Since there was no exit from the sea, they were doomed to float endlessly in aimless circles. But, as I recall, life went on as usual. That is, men fought among themselves over too few women and a dwindling supply of liquor and cigarettes.

A hundred or so years ago, during the era of sailing vessels when derelicts were numerous and before they were systematically hunted down and destroyed as a menace to navigation, the Sargasso Sea may well have harbored a handful, if not hundreds, of missing ships. The schooner *Fanny E. Wilson,* for example, was abandoned near Cape Hatteras, North Carolina, in 1891. A year later she was sighted west of the Azores, i.e., in the Sargasso Sea. After another year she was reported off Cape Hatteras at the very same spot where she had been abandoned two years earlier.

The *Alma Cumminger,* another schooner, was sighted in the Sargasso Sea several times over a period of nearly two years.

Even more remarkable was the saga of the *Florence E. Edgett.* In 1902 she sailed from Saint John, New Brunswick, with a cargo of timber, destination Buenos Aires. The *Florence* ran into one of the numerous gales to be encountered off Cape Hatteras and was dismasted, but not abandoned. For a month ship and crew drifted around the Sargasso Sea, hoping to be rescued. Finally, captain and crew abandoned her and arrived in Antigua after an exhausting eleven-day voyage in a lifeboat. The *Florence* was subsequently sighted in the Sargasso Sea in 1912—yes, ten years later! This confirms that derelicts can indeed drift within the boundaries of the Sargasso Sea for years, if not forever.

This sea of weeds is an oval-shaped area whose boundaries are, roughly, 20° N. latitude in the south, 35° in the north, and 2,000 miles from east to west in between, that is, from west of the Azores to east of the Bahamas.

Columbus, on his first voyage to America, passed south of the Azores and two days later sailed into a sea of weeds. Not surprisingly, his men thought the weeds were a kind of coastal kelp and expected momentarily to run aground. In fact, the bottom was some two and half miles beneath them.

The sargassum weed was named by Portuguese navigators who thought that its air-bladder floats resembled the small Sargasso grapes that were delicacies in their native land.

Probably most of us think of the Gulf Stream as

being a massive river of warm water flowing north along the American East Coast, then veering northeast until it nears and warms Ireland, England, and western Europe. Not so. The Gulf Stream goes no farther east than the Azores, where it breaks up. One minor branch does head north toward the British Isles, but this doesn't warm England by even one degree. The main branch heads south where it is called the Portuguese Current; this in turn melds with the North Equatorial Current, which is the one that is helping me along now. These then are the forces that compose the gyre that defines the boundaries of the Sargasso Sea.

The British Isles and western Europe are warmed by the westerly winds blowing over the warm Sargasso Sea. That is to say, the vast sea to the right of the Gulf Stream is warm, about the same temperature as the Stream itself. Even if the entire Gulf Stream reached northwest Europe it would exert little influence on weather of that huge region. The much more vast Sargasso Sea can and does create the mild weather conditions that the British Isles and to a lesser extent western Europe enjoy.

Midnight—The black moonless night drifts slowly away until it disappears in the luminescent wake. Or so it seems to me as I sleepily scan the invisible horizon for ships. When I go below to brew a now-precious pot of tea I look at the calendar and see that the new day will be the sixtieth alone at sea. For the past several days I have eaten nothing but spaghetti and, as a result, am growing progressively weaker. Nor is the fresh-water inventory encouraging. Less than a gallon remains, even though I have been drinking two mugs of sea water each day.

1:00 A.M.—A gentle breeze and clear sky, after squalls earlier in the evening. I should hoist the genoa, but for one thing I'm too tired. Furthermore, my stomach announces loudly that it makes sense to linger here awhile. In fact, I may drop the sails and wait for a ship to show up. Maybe I could barter spaghetti for real food.

The Marcos
from Manaus

A truer image of the world is obtained by picturing things as enter-ing into the stream of time from an eternal world outside, rather than from a view which regards time as the devouring tyrant of all that is. —BERTRAND RUSSELL

The flow of time is clearly an inappropriate concept for the descrip-tion of the physical world that has no past, present and future. It just is. —THOMAS GOLD

DECEMBER 8TH: This is the night I cannot afford to waste time sleeping. Food and water are more important. So I interrupt these recollections at ten- to fifteen-minute intervals to go out on deck and scan the horizon for ships. This is about the time a ship remains in sight after first appearing over the horizon. I am not very hopeful since I have not seen a single ship since turning west twenty-four days ago. At 3:30 A.M. I put on the teakettle, then step into the cockpit. I see a ship! It's some four or five miles off the port bow.

At sea, by definition, any light, where a short time

before there was none, must be coming toward you. I watch the light with the concentration of an alcoholic watching his last bottle, and conclude that she should pass relatively close to us. An hour passes and the ship is abeam but no closer. Strange! To make sure we are sighted I heave to and duck below for red flares. I tie two 36,000 candle-power giants to the stern pulpit and light them one after another. The flaming sky blinds me.

After a minute or so, when I am able to see again, I watch the ship for signals. The swell regularly obscures her lights, and I can't identify signals for sure. We are drifting slowly, i.e., one knot or less downwind, and I take a series of bearings on the ship with the hand-bearing compass. As far as I can tell, the lights are not moving. Strange indeed.

As the new day filters in with the wind from the east, the ship slowly becomes etched against the horizon to the southeast, about three miles away, and by now she is to windward. The swell has subsided and I can now clearly see her signal lamp flashing Morse code. I get out *Reed's*, since I don't know Morse, make up the message "I need food and water," and signal it over and over with the big torch.

Meanwhile, I write down the dots and dashes they are sending. After a while I realize they are sending single letters repeatedly. F and M. In the international code they translate "I am disabled, communicate with me" and "My vessel is stopped." Fantastic? I can't believe it. To come across a stopped ship? What are the odds against such an occurrence? Especially in this seldom-traveled region. But what a heaven-sent opportunity to replenish my fast-dwindling food and water.

The bent propeller shaft precludes motoring up to the ship, so I will have to approach her under sail, a prospect I do not relish. The history of such encounters teaches the need for the greatest caution in any near approach between a small sailboat and a large ship. I think of Harry Pidgeon and the many other singlehanders who have suffered damage to their boats in such encounters, especially the experience of Chichester in the transatlantic singlehanded race when a French weather ship, *France II,* approached *Gypsy Moth 5.* Sir Francis, who, unlike me, was adept at using Morse, signaled: "No aid needed. Thank you. Go away." He then headed *Gypsy Moth* in the opposite direction and went below. A few minutes later he heard a loud horn and scrambled out into the cockpit where, to his amazement, he saw *France II* overtaking him and only some fifty feet away.

As the big ship passed, it came too close and, before Chichester could take any evasive action, his mizzen mast smashed into the side of the ship and sheared off. The top of it became entangled in the backstay and was prevented from falling by the triatic stay that leads from the top of the main mast to the top of the mizzen mast.

After this display of negligent behavior, the *France II* steamed away to seek out another victim, which turned out to be the American yacht *Lefteria,* which was sailing south for the Caribbean with a crew of eleven aboard. According to the skipper, Philip Bates, at 1:00 A.M. on July 1 (twelve hours after the collision between *France II* and

Gypsy Moth) he saw the lights of a fairly large ship approaching from astern. He went on deck and signaled the weather ship, asking for their position. They signaled back, but he could not read it.

When the *France II* passed ahead and was well clear of the relatively slow sailboat, Bates returned below. Only two minutes later he was sitting at the chart table when the *France II* plowed into the *Lefteria,* hitting her amidship. Bates dashed out and was swept overboard. He and three others were picked up by the weather ship. His wife and six other crew members perished. If the testimony of Bates is to be believed, one can only conclude that the crew of the *France II* was either drunk or drugged.

So as I got under way I was well aware of the dangers involved. First, in order to beat to windward, I must dismantle the self-steering sail and gear. As it turns out, the breeze is more from the east than south, and I can just lay the stranger close-hauled on the port tack. An hour later I can make out her name, *Marcos Santos Dantos* from Manaus. Wherever that is.* For some reason I think it is in Africa. Perhaps because the crew who are watching and waving with friendly interest range from brown to black, including a handsome brown girl wearing a white T-shirt and shorts. I can see one white officer, who, judging from his cap, might be the captain. The *Marcos* is a large container ship with its lower row of portholes even with *Fidelio*'s spreaders.

---

* Manaus is a city in Brazil, situated on the Amazon River, some eight hundred miles from the Atlantic Ocean.

When we are less than a cable off, I ease the sheets. The captain speaks to a brawny black man who shouts something in English, which I can't understand. I, in turn, yell back, "I'm sixty days out of England and need food and water." Sign language leaves no doubt as to my meaning. The captain sends two of the crew below for, I hope, food and water. The black interpreter seems to be asking, "How many? Are you alone?" To which I nod, "Yes," hold up one finger, and shout, "Alone, solamente mio." This seems to impress them more than anything else.

Now they pick up lines with monkey's paws attached to the ends and indicate I should maneuver around to the stern where they would throw me lines. I shake my head: "No." I want to stay on the leeward side of the ship where the sails are windless and we can remain relatively stationary. But by now we are drifting away; so I haul in the sheets, wear *Fidelio* around and, after a few minutes, approach *Marcos* once again, closer this time. The crew immediately throw down lines to which I attach a two-gallon and a five-gallon water container. They haul them up and take them below to be filled.

Again I indicate my need for food and also hold a chart and ask, "What is your position? Longitude, latitude?" The captain heads for the bridge at once. Meanwhile, before I know what is happening, *Fidelio* gets sucked under the bulging hull of the *Marcos*. Our shrouds snap off a large ventilator, which crashes down on our deck, spraying rust everywhere. The port side spreader bends ominously, the upper shroud is fouled around something. I wonder, if this is the end of the line for *Fidelio*, should I board the ship and go to Africa or stay with *Fidelio* and ask them to radio for help?

Meanwhile, I am pushing off their hull with the strength of desperation, which isn't very much. Crew members are running above me from one porthole to the next, trying to free the shrouds and push *Fidelio* off. The grinding sounds are bloodcurdling, rust and paint pour down on us, along with canned goods and the two-gallon container filled with water, which I manage to cut free of their line just as we finally drift clear of the *Marcos*. They try to lower the five-gallon jerry can aboard, but it is too heavy and falls short.

The port spreader has survived as have the shrouds, although there is now a kink in the upper shroud just below the spreader. There is no question in my mind; if *Fidelio* had been rigged like most stock 32-footers we would have been dismasted. Instead, we begin to bear off as the sails fill. The crew of the *Marcos* beckon to me to return for more goodies they have now collected. I figure I have pushed my luck far enough. Instead, I doff my cap and shout "Muchas gracias" over and over. They are Brazilian, I see from a newspaper wrapped around a corned-beef can, and probably will understand Spanish.

I quickly rig the self-steering sail, then gather up the cans, which are mostly corned beef and Vienna sausages. Also wrapped around one of the cans is an old chart of the North Atlantic with the position of the *Marcos* plotted on it: 52° 44′ W., 16° 10′ N. This agrees perfectly with my own, a great relief. After all sixty days have passed since my last sight of land, and even a small cumulative error

might cause us to close a small island sooner than expected—or miss it altogether.

This news, together with the food and our narrow escape, lifts my spirits sky-high. True, the strenuous encounter leaves me weaker than ever, but I should regain
strength quickly on an all-meat diet. To get started I fry a
can of corned beef and eat it out in the cockpit as we
slowly sail westward over an indigo sea. The corned beef is
a welcome change to both my diet and my taste buds, but
what I really crave are fresh fruits and vegetables. A salty
diet is not a good one with a low water supply.

There is just enough breeze to offset the hot sun. The
Marcos remains visible all afternoon, evidently waiting for
help or working on her engines before she can resume her
voyage.

Does the sunset seem to be unusually lovely because
of our narrow escape or my full stomach? Greens spread
high overhead from the east and then fade away gradually
to pink and rose near the western horizon.

DECEMBER 10TH: A slight breeze this morning, so I
hoist the sails and, while doing so, notice a small bird circling round and round us. Finally he lands on the tiller.
He has a dove-gray breast and black wings. A baby shear-
water? I have no way of telling, because my bird book has
succumbed to the damp and has been thrown overboard.
Not that it matters. I never had much luck identifying
birds from the illustrations in that book. In any event, he's
a sassy little bird who soon moves into and takes over the
cabin. His favorite perch is on the clothesline over the
sink.

I still haven't caught any fish and I abandon all plans

for scraping the bottom. I am much too weak to lower and recover the dinghy. As for going overboard direct from the deck, I doubt if I have the strength to pull myself back on board, even with the help of the boarding ladder. Nor, realistically, do I have the strength to remain underwater very long while removing the barnacles and grass which adhere to the hull as if glued with epoxy.

Noon position: 54° 24′ W., 14° 37′ N. This places me 180 miles closer to Barbados than to Antigua. This equals a couple of gallons of water at my present rate of progress, which is more than I have left. However, going there would mean an extra five hundred miles added to my planned route to the Virgin Islands and Puerto Rico. Guess I'll sleep on this because we are going nowhere right now.

Deadly hot calm all afternoon. I'm sitting with my feet in a bucket of water watching dolphins and silvery fish leaping out of the water plus, as usual, dorados circling beneath us.

As I gaze toward the infinite, endless horizon, I realize that I am becoming obsessed with the concept of "mind over matter." Because, potentially, it can solve *all* our problems? Because it reduces supernatural religious phenomena to matter-of-fact, psychological terms?

I can understand, to a limited extent, what the mystics and the new physics have in mind when they talk about the illusionary nature of the physical world. But the new view of time is even more difficult to grasp and then, finally, to believe. Probably most of us view time as flowing like a river. The future flows down toward us from upstream, becomes the "now" moment, then flows on down into the past.

This view of time that assumes space and time to be separate and unconnected was the foundation of Newtonian physics. However, as Einstein discovered, time is a function of one's location in space. In other dimensions and planes of consciousness, events that in the third dimension are seen as happening in the past and future are happening simultaneously and continuously. Actually, they are not "happening," they simply "are." There is no past or future; there is only "now."

In other words, the illusion that time flows like a river in only one direction is a product of our three-dimensional reality. As we will see, insects and animals whose senses create one- and two-dimensional worlds live in a timeless reality as do the entities in the higher dimensional worlds. The natural habitats of human mind/spirit (or soul) are these higher planes of consciousness where time does not exist, and therefore, where the soul is immortal. This hypothesis of the new physics is so hard for most people to achieve, or even to comprehend, because of their preoccupation with the physical senses and sense objects.

Probably this is also true of most physicists who understand and apply the new reality in the laboratory but not in daily living where the old time reigns supreme. Believing and acting are not the same thing. However, at least one of them not only believed; he changed his life accordingly. When Einstein's oldest and dearest friend died, Einstein sent a letter to the surviving son and sister in which he wrote in part: "And now he has preceded me briefly [this was in 1955, the year Einstein died] in bidding farewell to this strange world. This signifies nothing. For us believing physicists the distinction between past, present and future is only an illusion, even if a stubborn one."

The new concept of time can be likened to a movie where past, present, and future are all there in one reel. You can if you wish arrange to see the beginning and the end at the same time. Hence, the precognitive abilities of those psychics who are able to tap into these higher dimensions of consciousness. Those of us who do not have psychic abilities must cultivate the ability to live in the eternal "now" moment if we are to transcend our three-dimensional reality. In this way we simulate and finally merge with the higher planes of consciousness.

An analogy, though an imperfect one, may help us understand these difficult new concepts of reality. One day when I lived in Spain, I was walking along a dirt road among the endless fields of carnations that are grown in the coastal regions of Catalonia. In the distance whitecaps ruffled the ordinarily calm surface of the Mediterranean Sea. I came across a column of ants climbing a vertical cliff until they disappeared into a hole at about eye level. Their perseverance was remarkable because, when nearing their goal, if the wind picked up, many ants would tumble all the way back down to the road where they would doggedly start back up. I gradually inserted my foot in the path of the marchers and soon they were climbing up and over my shoe.

A common-sense ant would probably view my shoe as an object similar to a block of wood or a rock. What if an Einstein among ants came along and told this ant, "Right above you is an omnipotent, supernatural power (from an ant's point of view) a billion times larger and more powerful than all the ants in our nation combined. Moreover, there are billions of these 'gods' on our earth." The ant equivalent of a new physicist might accept this proposition if his faith in the Einstein ant was sufficiently great. The common-sense ant would, of course, reject the idea out of hand. Why? Because it could not be proven in terms that an ant could understand. An ant exists on a one-dimensional plane. Anything as large and three-dimensional as man is beyond its grasp.

Similarly, the world of the dog is two-dimensional. Suppose Rover has just returned by jet from London. He tells his friend Barky, who has never flown, that 30,000 feet up in the sky are flying houses that can transport a dog 3,000 miles in six hours, a distance that would take a dog several months to cover. Barky would not only not believe it, he would not be able to comprehend his friend's statement.

Normal men and women, who exist in a three-dimensional world, are equally unable to comprehend a fourth, or higher, dimension in which powerful beings, spirits, entities, and gods exist, who can as profoundly affect our lives as we can affect the lives of ants or dogs. May we not be as blind, as wrong, as the common-sense ant and Barky, the dog? The mystics and new physicists think so and the longer this voyage lasts, the more I do, too.

Of course, I shouldn't imply that only mystics and new physicists see and believe in a higher-dimensional world where spirit reigns supreme. Numerous poets and philosophers, from Plato and Dante to George Berkeley, William Blake, and our own Emerson, have experienced the worlds beyond the five senses, as have numerous ordinary, undistinguished citizens.

In the eighteenth century George Berkeley argued in a series of books that nothing exists except by being perceived. Therefore, mind is the only reality, while matter is an illusion. Our physical world is a mental construct, a system of relationships created from experience to coordinate our perceptions of sight and touch. Interestingly, he was harshly critical of Newton's laws, which he knew intuitively were wrong! Shades of Bell's Theorem! Two hundred and fifty years ago Bell had a precursor in the form of an Irish bishop.

William Blake, who died in 1827, often sang about the unity of the universe. Within each of us there is a blueprint for the entire universe. Mind and matter are one. We are one with the universe. The form and structure of the entire world are contained within each part; we are all part of the whole.

Blake summed up these conclusions of the new physics in two couplets:

> *To see a World in a Grain of Sand*
> *And a Heaven in a Wild Flower,*
> *Hold Infinity in the palm of your hand*
> *And eternity in the hour.*

Emerson began his career as a teacher in a finishing school for young ladies, then became pastor of his parish church in Concord, Massachusetts, and finally at age thirty-two turned to the writing of poetry, essays, and lectures that established his reputation. He had no background or training in science. Nonetheless, parts of some of his essays could have been written by one of today's scientists, discussing the implications of subatomic physics. For instance, from "The Over-Soul":

> We live in succession, in division, in parts, in particles. Meanwhile, within man is the soul of the whole, to which every part and particle is equally related; the eternal One. And this deep power in which we exist and whose beatitude is all accessible to us, is not only self-sufficing and perfect in every hour, but the act of seeing and the thing seen, the subject and the object are one. We see the world piece by piece, as the sun, the moon, the animal, the tree, but the whole, of which these are the shining part, is the spirit.
>
> The spirit abolishes time and space. The influence of the senses has in most men overpowered the mind to that degree that the walls of time and space have come to look real and insurmountable; and to speak with levity of these limits is, in the world, the sign of insanity. Yet time and space are but inverse measures of the force of the spirit.

The renowned physicist Sir Arthur Eddington said the same thing in fewer words: "The stuff of the world is mind stuff."

THE NEW REALITY

The new physics has confirmed the claims of the mystics that there are higher levels of consciousness and dimensions of time and space that are as superior to our ordinary consciousness and reality as the Concorde is to the Wright brothers' first flying machine. How can we make contact with this new reality? By getting in tune with the mysterious power that runs the universe. The mystics tell us we can do this by concentrating the mind through meditation.

But first what exactly is this mysterious power? The important word here is "mysterious" because only those people who are united with it or plugged into it know, and they can only report that the experience is ineffable. We will label this power "God" because this is a familiar and short and largely meaningless word.

And so with this caveat, let's survey some definitions of this ultimate power that we label "God." We have the testimony of many avatars, mystics, and even ordinary citizens who tell us that they have seen God. Or, more accurately, that they have become united with God in that state of super or cosmic consciousness variously referred to as the kingdom of heaven, Nirvana, *samadhi*, ayin, and so on. Anyone who has carefully studied these accounts can only conclude that they describe identical experiences even though some of those reporting were men, some women; some lived in the East, some in the West; some lived in ancient times, some in modern times, and some in between.

Perhaps, this explains why their definitions of God

differ so widely. Then, too, the definitions must be couched in paradoxical terms if they are to convey any meaning at all to limited three-dimensional minds. Thus, we can say that God is both personal and impersonal, everywhere and nowhere, with form and without form, within us and outside us. This explains why God has been defined so variously: as spirit, love, ultimate reality, creator, divine ground, universal mind, and so on. God is all these and much more.

Sri Ramakrishna defined God as "Neti, Neti"—"Not this, not that"—which was his way of emphasizing that God cannot be defined in words used by mortals to conduct their daily business. Thomas Aquinas's definition: "God is a circle whose center is everywhere and whose circumference is nowhere." Meister Eckhart saw God as "the denial of all denials." An eighteenth-century Jewish mystic: "God is ever present, perfect joy." Some see or hear God as an inner voice of conscience.

The Buddha was one of the first to experience a higher level of consciousness, which he labeled Nirvana. He saw that the mass of men are caught in an existential trap of which they are not even aware. It seems self-evident that human love, material security, success, or whatever will lead to the goal they are seeking. However, life itself is transitory and we make demands on it that, by its very nature, it can never fulfill.

In fact, it is this faith in the efficacy of the traditional paths that, sooner or later, leads to despair and suffering. Most of us don't believe this as long as things are going along more or less as we think they should. But in due course, the day dawns when some part of our house of cards collapses. We then wake up and realize that we can escape from the trap only by abandoning our old path and finding a new one.

The Buddha was the first to believe what the new physics has proven: Mind creates and controls matter. One sentence of his can revolutionize our lives: "We are what we think we are."

What was the Buddha's program that leads to enlightenment?

Before spelling out the Eightfold Path, we should remember that he blamed human suffering on unrequited desires. Since *all* desires can never be gratified, we are caught in an emotional dead end of our own making.

How can we overcome desire? By developing compassionate detachment and discernment, by being aware of the interdependence and unity between the individual and the cosmos. Such awareness can be realized via meditation and constant mindfulness.

The Eightfold Path

1. RIGHT UNDERSTANDING: We all know that something is wrong, that something is lacking. Fame, money, power, success do not bring the fulfillment expected. This is because all worldly rewards are transitory. Believe that your mind can create a state of eternal bliss if you first free yourself from the tyranny of the ego and the bondage to ingrained negative thoughts.

2. RIGHT MOTIVE: This amounts to being true to yourself; sincere. Don't undertake any new course of action for the wrong reasons, i.e., the means are more important than the end. Loving and serving others must take precedence over loving and serving yourself.

3. RIGHT SPEECH: The Buddha endorsed Jesus' contention that every idle word we utter will build yet another barrier to attaining Nirvana. Not only should we monitor what we say, but also what we listen to. All senseless distractions are covered here.

4. RIGHT ACTION: The Christian Ten Commandments.

5. RIGHT LIVELIHOOD: Is my occupation morally or otherwise harmful to myself or others? Few are inclined to answer "Yes." The Buddha left it up to the individual. Here are his words: "Does it [your occupation] conduce to the harm of self, to the harm of others, to the harm of both? Is it wrong, productive of ill, ill in result?" If the answers are yes, or even maybe, then "work such as this should not, as far as you are able, be done by you."

6. RIGHT EFFORT: Every effort must be made to eliminate negative thoughts and emotions; to encourage positive thoughts and emotions. Perseverance is all-important. Pursuing the Path must take precedence over every other activity.

7. RIGHT MINDFULNESS: Be constantly recollected. In Christian terms, think only of God. Practice the presence of God as you do your daily work and play. Seek out people who have similar spiritual goals.

8. RIGHT MEDITATION (or *SAMADHI*): The Buddha told his followers that to meditate effectively they must first banish "lust for the corporeal, lust for the incorporeal, pride, excitement, and ignorance." He then describes the four stages of meditation in which the mind becomes progressively more "concentrated and one-pointed." If you persist you attain Nirvana, or what Western mystics refer to as the unitive knowledge of God.

In contrast to the Eightfold Path, normal, worldly people are always doing and progressing restlessly from here to there, from now to then. The "there" is more important than the "here," the "then" than the "now."

The world rejects a philosophy of being for one of becoming to such an extent that the very idea of a static, timeless state of bliss is not only inconceivable, it is actually repellent. The universal desire is for continual excitement, change, and novelty.

In short, timelessness or eternity—like Paradise itself—is formidable and strange because it exists beyond the daily world of the five senses. It cannot be grasped by reason or intellectual effort but rather by a surrender of these faculties to an unseen, unfathomable, omnipotent higher power, which can be visualized in the mind's eye only by artistic or poetic images.

The path is so hidden and difficult because it can be found only by those who have abandoned all the traits upon which worldly success and recognition depend. When success is achieved we are bound ever more tightly by it. Therefore, failure to achieve worldly success (or the ability to abandon it once achieved) can be one of the surest means of finding the path that leads to spiritual freedom and self-realization.

The Psychology
of Solitude

It is in solitude that I find the gentleness with which I can truly love my brothers. The more solitary I am, the more affection I have for them. It is pure affection and filled with reverence for the solitude of others. Solitude and silence teach me to love my brothers for what they are, not for what they say. Now it is no longer a question of dishonoring them by accepting their fictions, believing in their image of themselves which their weakness obliges them to project, in a pathetic effort to communicate. —THOMAS MERTON

DECEMBER 11TH: A decision has to be made today—whether to continue on to Antigua or head south for Barbados. The latter is the closer by about three days and by now I am as sick of a salty, all-canned-meat diet as I was, only a few days ago, of an all-spaghetti diet. It makes me terribly thirsty and I am again down to less than one gallon of fresh water. Nor am I regaining strength as rapidly as I had expected. Moreover, I am overdue. Kathy has had no word for more than two months and will be worrying, as only those who helplessly wait can worry. And wouldn't you know, the wind finally has the northeast slant I have been wanting for so long. However, it cannot be depended on, so I go below and plot a new course for Barbados. I find I can do it on the West Indies chart, which is most encouraging.

This part of the ocean swarms with life—porpoises frolicking, silver-scaled fish leaping twice their length out of the water, as well as the endlessly circling dorados. It's like the Florida movies of deep-sea fishing. Unfortunately, none of them is attracted to Vienna sausages. Evening falls like a gold-and-green curtain toward which *Fidelio* ghosts along, sails barely filling, water softly lapping at the bow. When the magic colors fade I go below and turn on the radio. Christmas seems to be an important holiday in the Caribbean. I listen to "Silent Night" and "White Christmas." The melody of the latter is familiar but the words have been altered to "Green Christmas."

DECEMBER 12TH: I'm sad. Came out on deck and discovered the little bird dead. It seemed lively enough last night, but refused to eat the meat I offered.

9:30 A.M.—Gybed again. And again Vienna sausage for breakfast, during which I finish one of the books that has survived the one hundred percent humidity and worse. It's *The Winds of War,* by Herman Wouk, about a navy family in World War II. The father is a battleship man whose ambition is to command one. Just when he is about to realize his ambition all the battleships are sunk at Pearl Harbor. One son is a flyer, the other in submarines. A marvelous story—deadly serious soap opera. This is the way it really was. At no time do the characters in the novel have any control over their actions. They are all robots reacting to events in whatever fashion they have been programmed. They *are* the labels that have been stamped on them since birth.

If I picture myself as a stockbroker, a soldier, or a butcher, and associate with and accept the social and moral values of brokers, soldiers, or butchers, then I automatically guarantee that I must live in a state of "self-conditioned somnambulism." The opposite state is one wherein you are in tune with Ultimate Reality as it presents itself from moment to moment and are, therefore, fully awake and alive.

Why must this be so? Because as soon as we label ourselves—and what the label is doesn't matter—we, thereby, accept the moral values of that label; i.e., we make a moral judgment. As Huxley says, "If I value an opinion because it is *my* opinion, or *my* political party, or *my* occupation, then I am always morally wrong and always closing the door on the liberating spiritual freedom which all men seek."

When we judge a person by his label, we do so because it confirms us in our attachment to *our* label. In short, our response is dictated by the label and, hence, is not spontaneous and free. To the extent that we manage to avoid labeling ourselves, we become alienated from and maladjusted to our society, if we are not judged to be actually insane.

Such was my wartime experience in the army. The military mind was so ludicrous that I laughed my way through basic training and was rewarded by being assigned to the medical corps. My job was taking case histories of surgical patients. This required no more than two or three hours a day and I had no other duties. Fortunately, the day room had a phonograph and an excellent selection of classical records. Here I spent most afternoons listening and reading. The evenings and often the entire night I devoted to the round-the-clock poker games that were the most memorable feature of life at Camp Crowder. After a few months I had built up a bank account sufficiently large enough to enable me to extend my gambling to the stock market.

In time this cushy job and dissolute life began to pall, so I applied for a transfer to the ASTP program, which the army had recently and thoughtfully introduced. The lucky men selected were sent to various universities, where they usually lived in fraternity houses requisitioned by the army. My first stint was at the University of Minnesota, where I arrived in time for the beginning of the Minneapolis Symphony season. Servicemen were given choice seats free of charge. Otherwise, my time was divided between the new student center, the gym, and the library. Theoretically, I was waiting for a group to assemble for training in advanced chemical engineering, but nothing ever came of it.

As it turned out the closest the ASTP program could come to my specialty was sanitary engineering. So now I headed for the University of Illinois, which offered such a course under Professor Babbit, renowned throughout the world for his profound books about sewage treatment.

I like to think that it was Professor Babbit, standing over his vats of sewage, who unknowingly arranged the meeting with my future wife on the yellow Milwaukee sleeper clicking through the icy winter night toward Chicago. There I would lay over most of the next day until the Illinois Central departed for Champaign-Urbana. At breakfast, about an hour before we reached Chicago, I was seated next to a beautiful young lady who, I quickly noted, did not wear a wedding ring. Her response to my small talk was cool, to say the least. In fact, she seemed considerably more interested in the snow-covered Illinois countryside than in me.

Later, walking down the platform, I managed to run into her again and when I offered to carry her bags to the taxi stand, her response was more friendly. No taxis were available, so we walked to the Palmer House, where she had a room reserved. Things moved fast in those days. In the five hours before my train departed we covered a lot of ground. I learned, among other things, that she worked for a New York auditing firm and traveled from one audit to the next. In fact, as my train pulled out of the station, I made a decision; perhaps it was the way the cold wind off Lake Michigan was blowing her hair. Anyway, the next day I phoned her in Davenport, Iowa, and suggested that we get married. She agreed.

A few days later I sat at a desk in one of Professor Babbit's classes beside a large tank of sewage and listened absentmindedly to what sounded like the purest shit: "Someday you young gentlemen will come to love all this as much as I do."

The sanitary engineering course was tough. Or so my roommate assured me. Night after night he slaved away, while I lay in my bunk writing love letters and poems. After two months, during which I never opened a book (about sewage treatment, that is), I was called into the presence of the commanding officer. Did I appreciate the consequences of flunking out? I did. It meant being reassigned to the infantry and going overseas. Admittedly, not an inviting prospect at any time, and especially not now when I was intent on getting married.

Equally unattractive (to me) was the reward for passing the course: officers' training school. Freedom varies inversely with rank. Thus, Napoleon, who should have known, said he had less freedom than anyone else in the world. He was supremely intelligent and realized that his every move was dictated by events over which he had very little control. In my case, I was damned if I did and damned if I didn't. The very next day a miracle rescued me, demonstrating the futility of worrying about the future.

Again I was called before the commanding officer, who looked at me as if I had grown an extra head. He had never before seen an order like this one. He handed me my copy. Reference was made to a number of secret telegrams and telephone messages. I was to proceed via the Illinois Central to Chicago, get off at the 54th Street station, and call the telephone number indicated. My papers were being forwarded to Oak Ridge, Tennessee.

I floated up to Chicago in a trance but managed to get off the train at the 54th Street station, went to a telephone, and dialed the number. A woman answered. I said, "Hello, this is Sgt. R. W. Bridwell calling; serial number 9384782." She replied: "Oh, yes, we were expecting you. Go out and wait in front of the station and my husband will pick you up shortly." This I did. In ten minutes a car stopped. The driver, a thirty-year-old man in civilian clothes, opened the door and said, "Hop in." We drove to his apartment, which was nearby. There I met his wife and two small children.

While we ate lunch he explained that I was being assigned to a top-secret project and gave me a round-trip ticket to my home in St. Joseph, Missouri, where I was to leave my army uniform and report back in civilian clothes. I was to carry no identification of any kind. In case of an emergency I should give the MPs or whoever was concerned the name of Major Black, who could be reached by phoning a number in Oak Ridge, Tennessee.

In reply to my questions, he said that he had no idea as to the nature of the project, which was doubtless true. As it turned out, of course, it was the Manhattan Project.

My point is this: If I had attached a label to my shirt on which I had printed "Buck and kiss ass to become an officer," and then made every effort to live up to that label, consider the probable outcome. I would have diligently studied Professor Babbit's books, as all of my classmates were doing so that they could pass the course and go on to OCS. Certainly I should have encountered no difficulty measuring up to the army's standards for officers, if the caliber of the second lieutenants I had run across reflected those standards. However, as a green, expendable lieutenant I would almost certainly have been sent overseas, where the mortality rate for second lieutenants was even higher than for sergeants.

So I decided to proceed on my labelless way, which was to write love letters and poetry rather than to wallow in the stench of sanitary engineering. The upshot was that I married Kathy, and lived with her in my homeland for the remainder of the war. Compare my story to that of

"Pug" Henry in *The Winds of War;* was it the same war? One thing is certain: He was more serious about it than I was.

A sobering thought: Isn't it because of humorless, labeled men like "Pug" Henry that the world may be destroyed at any moment by a nuclear exchange?

DECEMBER 13TH (FRIDAY): 10:30 A.M. I gybed again. Course 210°–220°. Walker log reads 4,365 sea miles. Breakfast: Vienna sausage again. This is all I have left except for one can from the *Marcos* which—judging from the picture on the wrapper—might be cannelloni, which will be a welcome change for dinner tonight.

This is the sixty-sixth day of complete solitude (except for the half hour I spent banging into the hull of the *Marcos*), so I try to analyze its effect on me. After all, I must now qualify as an authentic expert on the subject.

First, I suspect my reactions to this experience will surprise most people who would probably say, "Being alone sixty-six days would drive me up the wall." On the contrary, I have never felt so *sane,* so in tune with the essence of all life. From this I deduce that insanity is a product of society, sanity is a product of solitude.

The psychology involved is quite simple. Society suffocates us with its pressures, artificialities, and omnipresent distractions. Society feeds on itself to the point where it dictates or dominates, either overtly or covertly, every aspect of our thought and behavior. And this ever-present Big Brother systematically tries to block rather than encourage each individual's struggle toward self-realization.

Society resembles the army in one respect: It tries to reduce everyone to the lowest common denominator.

When I went through basic training in the army, I observed that those who didn't drink, smoke, swear, or tell or listen to dirty jokes were not accepted as "one of the boys." This pressure was so powerful that some of the more sensitive men couldn't cope and were, therefore, discharged under the "Section Eight" rule, i.e., they were unable to adjust mentally to the standards of the army.

Society is the same in that it exerts continual pressure on us to buy products we don't need, bombards us with tasteless, mindless advertising, constantly stimulates our sexual appetites, assaults our ears with an ever-rising crescendo of noise, and so on. In a nutshell, society encourages us to be more rather than less greedy, lustful, and envious. When one automatically responds to all these stimuli without discriminating, which is what most of us do, one tends to become a robot.

When society is collectively composed of robots (notably in the top echelons of government), rather than people who value their interior solitude, it can be held together only by the use of violent and abusive power. This produces collective resentment and hate (symbolized by nuclear weapons) rather than the inner serenity and love that are the fruits of interior solitude.

Our response to these pressures is to increase the time we devote to pointless activities, which we are unable to abandon because they enable us to avoid confronting our innermost selves. We seek refuge in pointless activities because we fear boredom more than anything else, even more than the IRS or death itself. These pointless activities include almost everything "normal" people do when they are not working at their money-making jobs or businesses.

Some of these activities may be relatively harmful (narcotics, alcohol, smoking); most are relatively harmless by the standards of society (spectator sports, television, cocktail parties, etc). However, no one attains self-realization by adhering to the standards of society. Instead, a new standard must be adopted. Does what I am doing make me a better or worse person? Does what I am doing have timeless significance or am I doing it merely to "kill" time? All the time I "kill" represents progress away from rather than toward self-realization.

Except for reading and very limited use of the radio (my supply of batteries was not unlimited), none of the usual activities and recreations had been available to me. As a result, I was never lonely as when alone in a big city and physically surrounded by strangers. As I mentioned earlier, I felt that my friends and family, including those departed, were physically as well as spiritually with me on the boat.

Was I impatiently counting the days, then hours until I could return to the pleasures and temptations of civilization? No. Despite the dangers and discomforts, one part of me wanted the voyage to continue indefinitely, suspended in the Now moment beyond time.

The other part of me would likely return to the somewhat different world of writing books and speculating in the stock market. I would, however, be able to view these activities with greater detachment, since I now understood the meaning of a sentence I read thirty-five years ago in the library of the University of Missouri. A Zen master told a student, "Nothing really matters simply because nothing really matters."

I pondered that message wistfully, yearning to embrace it. But I couldn't because at twenty-one everything mattered enormously and I didn't want to be free of those things that mattered most. For example, if my girl friend had a date with someone else I was literally sick with jealousy. Before an exam I had butterflies in my stomach. Afterward, if I didn't get the grade I expected, I was filled with gloom, and so it went.

The Zen master was telling his student, "Don't take anything seriously except God; nothing else matters. When we cease to take things seriously we are no longer slaves to our passions and material security."

Even God should not be taken *too* seriously. This is why Ramakrishna told his devotees, "God is fun, join in the fun," and "God is joy, God is laughter."

He wants to free us from our belief that worldly activities matter. He wants us to see that as long as we try to alter things to conform with our idea of how they should be, we are not free and ready for union with Him. So long as we *care*, we are not free. We are placing our faith in the illusion from which we are trying to escape, rather than in Him.

On this voyage I think I have finally accepted the Zen master's formula for self-realization, *really* accepted it. As well as its corollary: If your faith is sufficient, *everything* that happens, happens for the best. Perhaps this is why during the last part of the voyage I have been recollected most of the time. That is, I felt the presence of God in every part of my being, in every cell of my body, in the sea around me, in the heavens above, in the birds and the sea creatures. And I could feel myself in all of them. We are all one and the same essence of immortality.

I felt compassion and love for these creatures and for my fellow men, which often brought tears to my eyes. Or, an intense spiritual mood might come over me by thinking, for example, of the dying Christ saying to the thief on the cross beside Him, "Today thou shall live with me in Paradise." At such a moment I would willingly change places with that thief and consider myself the most fortunate of men.

Being constantly recollected while leading an active life in the world is something else. However, it can be done. We all know at least one or two people who radiate that inner serenity that reveals the presence of God.

How can we turn off the ceaseless, idiotic monologue going on in our unregenerate minds and replace it with the continual inner prayer, or the state of being recollected that leads to the unitive knowledge of God? The answer can be found in one of the great classics of devotional literature: *The Practice of the Presence of God*. We can only wonder at the unusual beauty of this collection of letters when we learn that the author, Brother Lawrence, was an uneducated peasant who lived in Paris in the seventeenth century. As a young man he served in the French army, and thereafter as a household servant.

Then at age fifty-five he entered a Carmelite monastery, where he worked in the kitchen for the rest of his life. He intensely disliked his menial kitchen chores which, doubtless, helped him overcome this dualistic failing and attain sanctity. Even a dishwasher can become a saint if he can sincerely believe and pray that his work is for and pleasing to God. Brother Lawrence wrote these letters at the request of his abbot and against his will, because he was much too humble to think that he could have anything worthwhile to say about mystical theology.

In one letter he tells the august recipient, the Cardinal de Noailles M. Beaufort:

I renounced, for the love of Him, everything that was not Him, and I began to live as if there was none but Him and me in the world. Sometimes I considered myself before Him as a poor criminal at the feet of his judge; at other times I beheld Him in my heart as my Father, as my God. I worshipped Him by keeping my mind in His holy presence, and recalling it as often as I found it wandered from Him.

I found no small pain in this exercise, and yet I continued it, notwithstanding all the difficulties that occurred, without troubling or disquieting myself when my mind had wandered involuntarily. I made this my business as much all day long as at the appointed times of prayer; for at all times, every hour, every minute, even at the height of my business, I drove away from my mind everything that was capable of interrupting my thought of God.

Here we have Brother Lawrence's secret: "Every hour, every minute." And also: "I found no small pain in this exercise, and yet I continued it." Every spiritual teacher who has attained the Nirvana of self-realization assures us that if we will only persist and not give up we will eventually reach the goal. The great masters go further and tell us that the path *is* the goal.

6:00 P.M.—A big moment. I've been looking forward all day to opening this last can. What a disappointment! Are there such things as "hearts of palm"? Anyway, it's some sort of fibrous or root plant. Oh, well, cut up and fried with leftover Vienna sausage, it is not too bad.

Am washing the dishes when I realize that the wind is backing, which according to the pilot means an "easterly disturbance" might be on the way. It's not on the way, it's here! I just get the sails down in time.

10:00 P.M.—The squalls have retreated to the horizon but it looks like a wild, windy night. I can't pass up this favorable twenty-knot-plus gusty wind, so I get under way with only the steering sail and the reefed main.

The Sixty-eighth Day

Swiftly, swiftly flew the ship,
Yet she sailed softly too;
Sweetly, sweetly blew the breeze
On me alone it blew.

Oh! dream of joy! is this indeed
The lighthouse top I see?
Is this the hill? Is this the kirk?
Is this mine own countree?
                    —COLERIDGE

DECEMBER 14TH: 5:15 A.M.—Looked out and was startled to see the lights of a ship fairly close off the port bow, heading north on a course that would just about intercept us. I shine the torch on the sails and am relieved to see her alter course to pass about a cable astern of us. This is the first night I have turned on the masthead light since starting across. About time, too.

For breakfast I fry the last of the Vienna sausages. After brewing a pot of tea there is only a quart of fresh water left. For the first time in a month, I turn on the RDF set and it works! Moreover, I can hear a faint signal exactly where Barbados should be, about sixty-five miles southeast of here. I get busy and construct a chart of Barbados on the Baker plotting sheet, based on the description and distances given in the West Indies Pilot.

Finally, as the sun sets, I can hear in the east the welcome sound of wind rippling across the ever-receptive sea. Soon we are hurrying along steering a course that should wind up ten miles east of Barbados. For obvious reasons I want to make a landfall well to the east of the island, which is surrounded by coral reefs. At midnight I can see the loom of lights on the horizon to the southwest, just to the right of our course. It could only be Barbados, twenty or thirty miles off. Certainly far enough not to worry about piling up on reefs for a while. So I head for my bunk and, surprisingly, even though I am excited, fall into a deep sleep. At 3:00 A.M. I awake with a start and dash out on deck. Individual shore lights are now clearly visible! And they look close. The first sight of land in sixty-seven days? A thrilling moment.

After examining the coastline for an hour, I am thoroughly confused. Off to the right among low overhanging clouds, I can make out the loom of what seems to be two fifteen-second flashes, North Point. But, if so, the light at Kittridge Point, the easternmost point of Barbados, one flash every fifteen seconds, should be right in the middle of the shore lights, so plainly in view. There is no sign of it. I heave to and wait for daybreak. I try to sleep but, as usual, am thirsty. But not for sea water. Now that land is in sight I go berserk, get up, and hardly pausing for breath, drink all of my remaining fresh water.

DECEMBER 15TH: I have no detailed chart of Barbados, but I know Bridgetown is located on the southwest shore of the island a few miles north of South Point. The pilot describes the harbor in some detail, but for the elucidation of large ships rather than small yachts. What if the harbor resembles Shoreham or Weymouth, where sailing in would be impossible or extremely chancy? Well, whatever lies ahead, the one thing I won't need is the self-steering sail and gear. I can't even tack with it in place. So as the sixty-eighth day dawns, I dismantle it all, stow it below, break out the anchors and prepare them for action. In my weakened condition these preparations take nearly two hours before I am finally finished. Normally, it would require half an hour.

Meanwhile, about ten miles to the west, the mist-shrouded cliffs and rolling green hills of Barbados are calling. Under the big jib and main we head on a broad reach for the last headland I can see to the southwest. Noon comes and passes. Thirsty and exhausted I am steering under a broiling sun with my feet in a bucket of sea water. A couple of miles to the north I can see large seas breaking on the Cobbler reef. This is the most dangerous reef along the east coast. Barbados is a coral island (unlike most islands in the Caribbean, which are volcanic), and reefs surround it between a half mile and a mile offshore.

Now I see one of the typical Barbados fishing boats with open cabin and enormous long tiller. I wave for them to come alongside, and head up with sails flapping. They alter course, reel in some lines, and soon two smiling, black fishermen are alongside. Being sixty-eight days out of England didn't seem to register with them. But when I say I need water, they catch my container and quickly fill it from one of their own. One of them, judging the gyrations of the heaving boats perfectly, jumps nimbly aboard *Fidelio* and hands it to me. After drinking my fill, I remember a can of corned beef I had hidden for an emergency, so I go back below and fry a pan of it for the three of us. When they bring part of a stalk of bananas aboard, I unselfishly give them my share of the corned beef and gorge on their bananas.

The wind is light, progress slow. Beyond what I assume must be South Point, more land looms in the distance. We must have been farther north than I figured. To help pass the time I leaf through an ancient book on the slave trade, which I picked up in a secondhand bookstore on the Isle of Wight. Most of it has disintegrated, but parts are still readable. It concerns the slave ship *Ruby*, which made a landfall at Barbados on the evening of June 27, 1788.

Probably the weather was as delightful then as it is right now, at least in the shade of the sails, but not below decks of a slaver. The author was surgeon on the *Ruby*, which suggests that conditions might have been above average for a slave ship, because few of them bothered to carry a doctor. However, on the best of slavers conditions were uniformly hellish, suffocatingly hot with practically no ventilation or sanitary facilities. The chained slaves lived week after week in their own vomit and excrement.

The treatment of any slave who showed any resistance at all to such degradation can hardly be believed. Thus, on the *Ruby* at least, punishment ranged from flogging women to decapitating men. Sick or injured slaves (fighting among the half-demented blacks was all too common) were thrown overboard while still alive. However, the endless, senseless brutality was by no means confined to the white slavers.

In Africa they were supplied by black traders who sold their fellow countrymen into captivity. These black traders treated their black victims even more savagely than did the whites. An example: One boatload of prospective slaves that rowed out to the *Ruby* when she was anchored off the Guinea coast included a woman with a child in her arms. She was rejected because of her child and sent back to shore. Next day she was returned without the child. It had been killed the night before by the black trader, thereby removing the obstacle to the sale.

4:00 P.M.—Finally, we are rounding South Point. Now the trade wind blows across the island with a sweet, spicy odor of flowers, earth, and sugar. Truly heavenly. I can see the Barbados Hilton and an enormous tanker, which seems to be anchored out in the ocean. At 6:00 P.M. we round the southern tip of Carlisle Bay. With the setting sun behind us we sail close hauled into the crystalline turquoise-colored waters.

I breathe a sigh of relief when I see the straight approach to the anchorage where dozens of yachts are visible. Evidently, transient yachts anchor in the bay rather than in the harbor. When near the outermost yachts, I head up and slowly lose way. I drop the plow anchor with all available chain into about thirty feet of transparent water. It won't take hold, and I spend another weary hour jockeying *Fidelio* around before (I hope) it has set. Finally, I can sit down, overcome by fatigue and emotion. Then I remember the log. I haul it in and write down the reading: 4,552 sea miles, or about 5,235 land miles.

Am I offering up prayers of thanksgiving for the safe landfall after sixty-eight days alone at sea? No, I'm thinking about food. I'm thinking about fresh fruit and the famous Barbados rum. In fact, I'm thinking about rowing ashore in violation of customs regulations, when a customs launch, seeing my quarantine flag flying, chugs by and tells me that I will receive clearance at 9:00 A.M. Meanwhile, I'm not to go ashore or visit any other yachts, which I had been thinking of doing. I decide to comply; one more night doesn't matter. Besides, I doubt if I am strong enough to launch the dinghy.

The launch powers off, heading for Bridgetown and home. I sit bemused, looking across Carlisle Bay toward the western horizon, which is still streaked with reds and greens. The innermost "me" seems to be floating off into some ethereal realm where time does not exist. I have truly lost touch with the everyday reality of my fellow men, anchored to their narrowly circumscribed realities. The endless ocean, the pink beach, now invisible, the lights blinking on at the nearby Holiday Inn, where a band is warming up, seem like a dream. Or am I light-headed due to hunger and a month or more without any fresh food?

After sixty-eight days of constant vigilance, I can relax at last. What a glorious feeling! I climb in my bunk and sleep like a baby, safe at last in its mother's arms.

EPILOGUE

*Across
the Caribbean*

Tired of Paradise?

Who doth ambition shun
And loves to live i' the sun,
  Here he shall see
  No enemy
But winter and bad weather.
               —SHAKESPEARE

DECEMBER 16TH: Sure enough, at 9:00 A.M. the harbor master's launch filled with young black men in uniform ties up alongside, and most of them come aboard. They are curious but courteous, examine my passport, clearance papers, health-record book, and so on. Everything is in order except that my smallpox shot has expired and I must get a new one.

I ask them for help in launching the dinghy and they have it in the water in a minute. Then they insist on towing me to shore, although I feel quite capable of making it on my own. Near the beach they cast off the tow line. I row the remaining distance, where a beach boy from the yacht club helps me pull the dinghy above the high-water mark. He then formally introduces himself as Frank Eden. We shake hands on it. I walk unsteadily up to the Royal Barbados Yacht Club, where I fill my cans with water and carry them back to the dinghy.

Shaky as I am, I want to walk, walk, walk, *on land!* But not for long; I'm too hungry. I head back to a small store near the beach where I see such wonders as grapefruit, bananas, eggs, bread, and Mount Gay rum. I load up with as much as I can carry and barely make it back to the dinghy. Fortunately, Carlisle Bay is calm and quiet. I launch the dinghy and get myself and groceries safely away from the beach. The bay is protected from the ever-present trade winds, but if a swell is running out at sea, sizable waves roll ashore in the bay. At such times landing or launching the dinghy must be managed with great care to avoid swamping.

After gorging on fruit, freshly baked bread liberally spread with butter, and a mug of rum and Coke, I frost the cake by lighting up my first pipe in six weeks. Profound thoughts occur to me. I have missed tobacco more than alcohol and alcohol more than sex. Appropriately, at this moment I notice a dinghy approaching, rowed by a shapely "guapa chica" in a yellow bikini. I help her aboard and, surprisingly, she has already heard that I am alone and planning to head north.

She is Swedish and crewed across from the Canaries on the neighboring German ketch. She offers to ship out with me, citing her ability to cook and perform other useful functions. I am tempted and flattered, but equivocate.

After all, I need to recuperate and repair the motor and self-steering gear, which will require a matter of weeks rather than days. Meanwhile, if another opportunity to escape presents itself she should take it. And, as a matter of fact, only a few days later she marries the owner of a French yacht and sails away with him. Quick action, to say the least!

This is the first of many such offers from both men and women. During my stay in Barbados, an average of two or three yachts a week arrive, usually from the Canaries, and after hearing about their crew problems, I am happy to be a singlehander. The Canary Islands and Gibraltar are evidently teeming with transients seeking free passage across the Atlantic. Mostly attractive young people, Europeans seeking adventure away from home and Americans who have, often, run out of money. They offer to work for their passage and, sometimes, bring their own food and drink. The attractive-sounding arrangement seldom works out, at least not from what I observe. All too often, even crews who know each other well and have planned the voyage together are no longer on speaking terms when they arrive in Barbados. As soon as they land they can't wait to separate and depart, with someone else.

10:30 P.M.—I'm sitting in the lounge of the Holiday Inn, in a motionless chair with a drink on a motionless table. It makes me dizzy! In the moonlit bay I can see *Fidelio,* and even she is almost motionless for a change.

It's 6:30 P.M. in California so Kathy should be home from work. She answers the phone and becomes quite emotional when she hears my voice. When she recovers she is still confused. "Barbados? Where's that?" She had almost given up hope of ever seeing me again. The waiting and suspense was tougher on her than the sailing was on me, which makes me feel guilty.

Anyway, she thinks she can get an indefinite leave of absence on the 21st. She will fly here and I'm to phone her tomorrow night to confirm it and get details of her arrival.

DECEMBER 19TH: For three days I've done nothing but eat, drink, smoke, swim in the turquoise waters of the bay, and read the Sunday *New York Times* (five dollars). I walk all the way into Bridgetown for it, then buy fresh fruit and other tidbits at the farmers' market, more Mount Gay rum at the distillery outlet store, then return by bus with my loot.

I guess what I have been through justifies three days of sheer laziness. But enough is enough. *Fidelio* needs much maintenance and cosmetic work. So begins a program of painting, oiling the teak, searching for deck leaks and so forth. It progresses slowly. Cruising people are friendly, so most of the time seems to pass in visiting from boat to boat. A party nearly every night. As glasses are filled and refilled (a fifth of Mount Gay rum costs two dollars), all the tales and past experiences grow more and more fantastic. After all, none of your audience was present when the events you describe took place.

Nonetheless, I manage to find a diesel mechanic who comes up with a new propeller shaft and has sufficient ingenuity to install it without hauling the boat. We also hoist the engine and replace the bolts which had sheared off. Another black entrepreneur scrubs the bottom for fifteen dollars, which seems like a bargain to me.

Even luckier, today an English yacht anchors nearby, and it turns out they not only have Hydrovane self-steering but also have a spare rudder that they generously agree to sell. My luck is not so good when it comes to replacing the spinnaker pole. I look everywhere but cannot find a suitable replacement; not that it really matters because the passage to Puerto Rico should range mainly between a close and a broad reach.

I have become quite friendly with the black yacht-club employee who helped me with the dinghy the day I arrived and was too weak to pull it above the high-water line. Frank speaks English with the accent of a BBC announcer, as do all Barbadians. He is thirty and reminds me of O. J. Simpson. He rows out frequently to visit and one night I invite him to stay for dinner, which he seems to relish; salad, French bread, tuna-noodle casserole, and a bowl of grapefruit and bananas for dessert. While I think he is sincere in his friendship, he does have an ulterior motive. He wants to leave the island—all the local people I know have the same ambition. Specifically, when I sail away he wants to sail with me.

I explain to Frank that the skipper of a yacht is responsible for each crew member he brings into a port. Many skippers who sail across the Atlantic don't realize this. The skipper who arrives with a crew of three must guarantee the departure of three. If an incompatible crew member wishes to depart from the island by other means, it's the skipper who has to foot the bill.

Most countries require that the prospective visitor must have a certain minimum amount of cash when he arrives, and also a ticket *back* to where he came from. All these rules are not theoretical. The harbor police, at least here in Barbados, check departing yachts and if the number of crew departing adds up to fewer than the number arriving, the skipper is liable to be fined. Moreover, my wife is arriving day after tomorrow and she is all the crew I want or need on the short hop to Puerto Rico. Frank takes what is probably an often-experienced rejection with the cheerful good humor that seems charactertistic of these newly independent but poverty-stricken islanders. In fact, he invites us to his house for Christmas dinner, an invitation that I accept with sincere gratitude.

DECEMBER 21ST: Kathy's flight arrives at 4:00 P.M! I take the bus to Seawell Airport, which is on the other side of the island, but we ride back in a taxi through the waving fields of sugar cane and the farmhouses surrounded by their ubiquitous banana trees. Our reunion is joyous, but she is shocked by my emaciated condition. I couldn't visualize returning at once to the primitive austerities of *Fidelio,* so we check into the Holiday Inn for a week. This is even more of a treat for me than for her, since I have now been sleeping and eating on the boat for six months. *Fidelio,* deserted now, swings to her anchors in front of our hotel windows.

At dinner looking out over the bay where the lights of Bridgetown dance in the ripples, we laugh at our recent worries. For example, she had phoned the Coast Guard in Miami to report me overdue and asked them to start a search. Then she couldn't answer a single one of their questions, except to tell them the date of the last letter she had received and my destination. Their questions: size, color and description of *Fidelio*; type of engine, amount of food and water on board; the displacement; planned stops; radio communication; among other things. Their implication was that I had deliberately disappeared and that she probably wouldn't hear from me again. They had a point, since we had been separated by an ocean and a continent for eighteen months. In short, they weren't about to put out an S.O.S. to all ships at sea. No wonder she was delighted to be able to call them back and tell them that I had arrived safely in Barbados.

DECEMBER 25TH: The second Christmas in thirty years that we didn't decorate a tree; last year when I was in England was the first. Anyway, this is not the custom on Barbados; where would they get the trees? At 5:00 P.M. we walk the few blocks to Frank's house, which is a typical unpainted frame cottage surrounded by weeds and a few withered banana trees.

Inside, the furnishings are sparse but clean and neat. Frank introduces us to his wife and sister, who lives with them. Three or four children are playing in the backyard. We discuss the yacht club whose members, according to Frank, are all white, a remarkable coincidence on an island that is ninety-five percent black. Could the black governor of Barbados join the Royal Barbados Yacht Club if he wanted to? Frank doesn't know. I don't know, or care. I am more interested in another rum drink and dinner, which turns out to be delicious: salad, barbecued chicken, a tasty casserole of rice, tomatoes, and black-eyed peas, and pineapple for dessert. The three of us eat alone. His wife, sister, and children eat later.

The next day Kathy asks a question that answers itself. Why should we pay eighty dollars a day for this room when we have a floating home of our own out there? The relative isolation and quiet of *Fidelio* is a welcome relief from a hotel filled with noisy vacationers, mainly Americans and Canadians. While we can still hear the dance band, at least it is not as deafening out here. Also we find the company of other "yachties" much more compatible than that of the shoreside tourists.

Nearly three more weeks pass before I feel strong enough to haul up the anchor and head across the Caribbean.

The beauty of all these islands, the perfect climate, are incontestable, but I feel no desire to stay on any of them. Paradise quickly palls; a cultural vacuum develops for emigrants from America or England, most of whom can't return home soon enough. Perhaps my reaction is aggravated by comparison with London and its endless variety of historic, artistic, and musical attractions. Another reason for this feeling of a cultural vacuum might be the fact that talented natives migrate to Europe or America as soon as they can arrange to get away. Or possibly, they want to escape the high cost of living. Brown sugar, rum, and bananas are about the only bargains. Even allowing for the fact that home heating and winter clothing are unnecessary, all other necessities cost twice to three times as much as in England or America. Yet wages are not higher. The local residents seem to manage by growing or catching (in the sea) a large part of their food requirements and by doing without such American necessities as the automobile, television, and movies.

Bird Island

The world is now too dangerous for anything less than Utopia.

—BUCKMINSTER FULLER

JANUARY 14TH: All my life I have dreamed of living on a tropical island, and Barbados exemplifies the best of all I have imagined. Perfect climate (if you like it on the hot side), coral beaches, and friendly people. So here I am impatiently waiting to sail away. All the partying is fun at first, but it too soon palls. As does carrying groceries and other supplies from store to bus, from bus to dinghy, from dinghy to boat.

I am also thinking about that entry I made in the log off Cape Finisterre. I guess sailors are like women in labor who vow 'Never again." Then, in retrospect, they forget the fear and pain when they look at their babies. Similarly, when I look at *Fidelio* I think, "Weren't we great to survive all those gales."

10:00 A.M.—One reason I'm impatient: for an hour I've been unsuccessfully trying to break out the anchor. The bottom is visible but I can't see what is wrong. Steve, one of our new friends, who is skipper of the Alden 43, *Hacienda,* is a scuba diver so I start to relaunch the dinghy to seek his help. Happily, he sees our predicament and comes to our rescue before I get it in the water. He finds our chain wrapped around an old ship's anchor in forty feet of water and quickly untangles it.

Noon—We finally are motoring across Carlisle Bay, past three sugar-loading towers, past a white cruise ship, then steer due north. By 5:00 P.M. we are due west of North Point, smashing into the big swell rolling in from the northeast.

JANUARY 15TH: Last night was a long one and today seems endless as we pound north on a close reach under the storm jib and reefed mainsail. I would set out in January when the wind blows at maximum strength!

By evening we are about thirty-five miles off Martinique and the best course we can lay is 318° T. My plan is to go far enough north to cross into the Caribbean through the Guadeloupe Channel between Antigua and Guadeloupe, and then follow in the wake of Columbus, who on his second voyage coasted down the Leeward Islands to Puerto Rico. But now this would require a long tack out to sea to ensure ample sea room to avoid the reefs and islands off the east coast of Guadeloupe. Beating day after day into a Force-6 to -7 wind is no fun so I decide to cut through the Martinique Passage between Dominica and Martinique tomorrow, hoping to find smoother sailing in the lee of the island chain.

One of the mysteries of the seas occurred about two hundred miles north of our present position. In 1966, John Pflieger, founder of the Slocum Society, sailed alone from Bermuda and was nearing Antigua when he noted in his log that a large tanker was overtaking him. This was his last entry, and his sloop, *Stella Maria,* was later found abandoned with everything in order.

JANUARY 16TH: 9:00 A.M.—We tack and run downwind under the big jib on a new course of 250° M. *Fidelio* seems to be flying up and down the foam-crested waves. Kathy and I take turns steering for the sheer fun of it. Although both islands are mountainous and the channel is only twenty-two miles wide, no land is visible until 2:30 P.M. when the mountains of Dominica suddenly appear like ghostly citadels off the starboard bow. This is the southwest extremity of the island, which means my navigation has been perfect. By 5:00 P.M. a series of bearings indicate that we can lay a course of 300° M on the starboard tack to clear the island by about five miles.

The wind has increased to twenty-five, to thirty knots, so I replace the working jib with the storm jib, deep reef the mainsail, and head northwest with the Hydrovane once again in control. As we near the land, fierce gusts sweep down from the mountains of Dominica. Two waves sweep over *Fidelio,* carrying away the Walker log, and almost capsizing us! Water pours below through partially open hatches. The twelve- to fifteen-foot seas are interspersed with some that are much higher. To carry on against these williwaws seems foolhardy, so I drop the main, sheet the storm jib flat, and run downwind. By 11:30 P.M. only the loom of Dominica is visible, bearing 55°.

At midnight a most fantastic thing happens. I go out on deck to check lights directly ahead, doubtless fishing boats. I flash the torch on the tiller lines and notice the end of the preventer line dragging in the water. I pull it in and find the Walker log rotor and line wrapped around the preventer. At the end is the log itself, apparently none the worse for being washed overboard. By now the wind has risen to Force 8, gusting to 9. Some trade wind!

JANUARY 17TH: My courage returns with the new day's light, which, as usual, moderates the blast somewhat. Nonetheless, the seas are now fifteen to eighteen feet or more, as a result of the gale-force winds during the night. At 7:00 A.M. we resume the battle, making slow going over the mountainous seas on a course 335° M. Tonight is a replay of the one before, with the wind as implacable but with the seas appreciably higher. At dusk I give up once again and we drift westward before the wind at two and a half knots over the water and possibly three and a half, including the current. This is much too fast since I want to pass to windward of Islas de Aves—the Spanish name—a group of low-lying, unlighted, uninhabited islands some seventy-five miles to the northwest. To slow us down I stream three hundred feet of 14mm terylene-and-nylon line in the form of a loop with a foam rubber mattress at the end of it. This does the trick

4:00 A.M.—We sleep together in the forepeak where the single bunks can be converted into one almost queen-sized bed. This arrangement makes me feel sorry for single-handers.

I am dimly aware that Kathy has gotten out of bed but drift right back to sleep. But not for long. She is shaking me and I'm wide awake when I grasp what she is saying.

"Rod, get up, I think there's a man in the cockpit!"

"My master mariner," I think as I lurch from handhold to handhold. At the companionway opening I look out into the orange-lit cockpit. There is no one there.

She exclaims incredulously, "I could have sworn that an old man in slicker and southwester was standing out there." Spooky!

She had gotten up to investigate the sound of footsteps on the deck above us—just as I had heard footsteps one night in the Bay of Biscay. Perhaps she has a more acute sensibility that enables her to see the ghostly pilot whose presence I so keenly felt that night but could not see.

Kathy is not fearful of the sea per se, but rather of the mysterious forces or presences she feels are all-encompassing, especially at night when it feels like living in a haunted house.

JANUARY 18TH: Wind and sea moderate somewhat at dawn's early light and, as usual in the gentle Caribbean, we resume course under the storm jib and ten rolls in the mainsail. When I calculate our noon position I end up with an impossible result! And at a time when we are headed directly for the dangerous Bird Island group. How close are we? I have no reliable idea, since we have been hove to for the better part of two days. Our DR position is largely guesswork. The sextant has been knocked about quite a bit so I assume it is to blame. I get out the spare sextant, an English plastic job that has never been out of its case. I check the alignment of its mirrors and index error, no easy task in a violent seaway. At 2:30 P.M. I take a series of afternoon sights. These results are also wildly impossible, even after checking and rechecking my calculations until the figures paralyze my eyes and brain.

The situation is disturbing, if not critical. Approaching these islands in the dark is out of the question. And I have no desire to do so even during the day, because the highest point is only twelve feet above sea level and un-charted reefs surround the islands. Seas breaking on their shores might be difficult or impossible to detect among the already breaking seas that stretch endlessly around us to the horizon. How close are the islands? How far to wind-ward of them are we? I don't know. I do know that to continue on our present course of 335° might prove to be a fatal mistake.

The only prudent action is to heave to and drift downwind until we are safely to leeward of Isles Aves. So at 4:00 P.M. I sheet the jib in flat and we are once again drifting to the southwest, trailing the mattress to slow us down.

According to the West Indies Pilot, the surest way to pinpoint Bird Island is by the sound of the hundreds of thousands of birds that inhabit it. They can be heard two or more miles offshore. Kathy keeps a close lookout from the bow pulpit all afternoon and evening. If she sees or hears birds dead ahead I will start the motor and head south. Just as twilight fades away beneath the western horizon, we can hear a chorus of bird songs off to the right. Faint but clear, thousands (or millions?) of invisible birds. We both shiver and I duck below for sweaters. Uncanny. An hour passes. The sounds of this garrulous colony gradually fade away. While we never saw the island nor a single bird, the near miss was well worthwhile; I now know our exact position.

Nevertheless, I am thoroughly frustrated. Originally, of course, I had planned to coast along the lee of the Leeward Islands, that is to say from Dominica to Saba, then on to Vieques via St. Croix. This is the route Columbus followed. He sighted Dominica twenty-four days after leaving the Canary Islands. This was early on Sunday morning (hence the name), the third of November, 1493. Unlike many of the islands that were denuded to grow sugar cane, Dominica is still heavily forested and must look very much as it did when Columbus saw it.

From Dominica he steered north to explore the area between there and the Bahamas, where he landed on his first voyage. In the space of two days he discovered many of the Leeward Islands. Finally, on November 14, 1493, he landed on present-day St. Croix, which he named Santa Cruz.

Here he had his first fight with the warlike and cannibalistic Carib Indians. While the Spaniards did not condone the Carib habit of eating their neighbors, they admired these Indians for their other virtues and liked them much better than the more peaceful and, therefore, apparently less courageous Arawaks.

It was here that the famous episode took place between Columbus's friend from Genoa, Michele de Cuneo, and the beautiful Carib girl ne captured during the encounter. When Columbus gave her to him to be his slave, he took her into his cabin and then relates: "She being naked, I conceived a desire to take pleasure but she did not want it and treated me with her fingernails in such a fashion that I wished I had never begun! Then, I took a rope and thrashed her well, upon which she uttered such screams as you have never heard. Finally we came to an understanding and after that she performed as if she had been brought up in a school of harlots."

The Final Ordeal—
and Sign

What happens after death is so unspeakably glorious that our imagination and feelings do not suffice to form even an approximate conception of it.
— CARL JUNG

JANUARY 20TH: For two days we have smashed our way north on a close reach, never able to fly more than the storm jib and deep-reefed main against the blustery northeast trades that relent only before and after the frequent squalls. But between squalls the sky is clear. Like now. Above our wake we watch the Southern Cross, which is a far more impressive constellation than I had been led to believe. Each evening it sinks lower and lower in the sky and soon will no longer be visible. On this run to the north I rarely look at the compass or even turn on its light. I judge our course by noting the distance between the mast and the North Star, which rises higher and higher in the sky with each succeeding night.

JANUARY 21ST: At 9:30 A.M. I take a longitude sight with the greatest care. This, combined with the noon latitude, enables me to calculate our position as of noon, and again it pinpoints us where I know we aren't—somewhere east of St. Croix! I finally think to check the chronometer. What an obvious oversight! This quartz crystal wall clock kept such accurate time across the Atlantic that I have gotten out of the habit of checking its rate against time signals. When I tune in WWV-Fort Collins I find it is fifteen minutes off! What caused this? Maybe the magnetic poles are beginning to reverse. If I remember rightly, this happens at intervals of about 70,000 years.

After all my fruitless hours of wrestling with navigational mathematics, the correct time quickly locates us twenty miles off Tuna Point, the southeast tip of Puerto Rico. Just then Kathy goes out on deck and calls down to me, "Land dead ahead!" I join her and sure enough I can see the steep mountains of Puerto Rico ahead. By 3:00 P.M. the light confirms our position. It's Tuna Point.

However, my goal is Fajardo, which is on the northeast coast, i.e., dead to windward. I hoped to close the coast well to the east of Tuna Point and just to the west of Vieques, an island off the southeast coast. Instead, at 5:00 P.M. we are two or three miles west of Tuna Point with half a gale of wind sweeping through the narrow Vieques Channel and on down the coast past Tuna Point. To short tack thirty miles upwind and in the dark is out of the question. To heave to and drift downwind would further aggravate the problem. To motor would entail twelve to fifteen hours of concentrated steering through an intricate, narrow, reef-infested channel when I am already dead tired. I decide to beat offshore twenty miles or so and then back to try and gain some much needed easting.

By midnight, steering 110° M, we are twenty miles offshore. A long black squall line fills the horizon to windward, then hurries toward us. When it arrives I assume it is just another squall, but in view of the ominous extent of the front, I drop the jib and sit on the cabin top beside the mast ready to pull down the main. Inky, ragged clouds fly by, then with a roar a hurricane force blast hits us. Almost simultaneously I release the halyard and haul down on the sail. When about one-third down it sticks, held as far as I can tell only by the force of the wind. The leech flogs with riflelike reports. To save the sail, if possible, I gather it up to the mast and wrap my arms around it and the mast.

Minutes and more minutes shriek past as I cling to mast and sail; actually, if I let go I think I would be blown overboard. Finally, during a slight lull, yanking with all my strength and weight I get the sail down and tied, after a fashion, to the boom. In the process I see that it has ripped along the leech clear up to the headboard as cleanly as though cut with a razor. How much wind could do this? I estimate the wind force at 10, gusting to 12.

Later, we learned that an Italian yacht had capsized at the same time and in the same area. When she righted she had a foot of water in her cabin.

I lash the tiller down and let *Fidelio* lie ahull. I don't want to run downwind and, thereby, give up whatever easting we may have gained. This should be safe enough because the waves are nowhere near the size of those in the Cape Finisterre gale, but not because of insufficient wind. They just haven't had enough time to build up. Below I cuddle up with Kathy in the forward bunk. Later she confides to me that she has no fear of the boat capsizing or the gale-force winds and rough seas, but every time I go on deck to change sails, she waits with bated breath until I return to the cabin and bed, although she often pretends to be asleep. She has great faith in my abilities to sail *Fidelio* through heavy weather, but has heard too many tales of yachtsmen being washed overboard, and this is her fear. However, she also has another problem: Her body is literally covered with bruises from being thrown about.

2:00 A.M.—Will this squall ever end? It has lasted much longer than any of the others. Why am I so surprised by the violent winds in this area? Didn't Columbus experience similar conditions? I get up, light the candle, and pull down my Columbus book. Sure enough, it was late October while nearing Dominica. A violent thundersquall, complete with the ghostly electrical phenomenon known as Saint Elmo's fire, struck the fleet in the middle of the night, ripping several sails and breaking several spars before sail could be reduced. It lasted four hours.

JANUARY 22ND: 4:00 A.M.—I can tell that the wind has moderated. I don gear and harness, go out in the dark, and head north with only the ripped mainsail set. Close-hauled on the starboard tack, smashing into the seas with spray flying over us, most of it going into the cabin or so it seems, sitting at the table with water dripping on my head.

6:00 A.M.—The sea is almost calm. Never have I seen

it subside, so quickly tranquilized by the first gentle breeze, since leaving Barbados. This presents the first favorable opportunity for breathing exercises and meditation. When I finish I'm ready for breakfast, but when I open the hatch I see Kathy is still asleep so I decide not to disturb her.

Instead, I get out the cockpit cushions and sit entranced by the magnificent panorama that is lighting up, glowing, unfolding out of the darkness. A few miles to the west the towering, ominous, black squall line is undergoing a chameleon change; luminous light is replacing the blackness like a curtain descending as the sun rises. The sunrise itself is like a painting by Turner. I compare it in my mind's eye to a famous Turner sunrise in the Tate Gallery.

The waves, too, have been transformed from dirty gray to outer-space blue. In the distance the mountains of Puerto Rico are bathed in celestial light. I see these physical objects as subtle vibrations of light and color. The blue ocean waves have become luminous billows of ineffable heavenly bliss coming toward me from all sides until I am drowning in them.

The breath is pulled out of my body, which has dissolved in this ocean of ethereal light stretching to infinity. First, I feel suffocated, choking on tears and emotion. This emotion is one of overwhelming joy and wonder, of final release and freedom. Now from this light, like nothing on earth, from another world, enveloping the boat, materializes an unsubstantial figure on the foredeck who begins speaking to me without using ordinary words. I have the same feeling of closeness and familiarity toward this entity that I had that night in the Bay of Biscay, when I was incapacitated and my ghostly pilot, invisible but palpably present, brought *Fidelio* safely through a terrible night.

"You are in the Paradise of humans this minute and every minute till the hour of your death, when you will enter the Paradise of the gods, which is located in astral regions the beauty of which is beyond your comprehension. This is why physical death is the most glorious, culminating experience of your earthly life. When you are ready, willing, and eager to leave this life at any time that you may be called, you are fulfilling your human destiny. Then and only then you triumph over all the human weaknesses and failings, then you comprehend the meaning of human life on earth. Your progress toward this final goal is measured by the extent to which you give yourself and your selfless love to any and every person you meet. This universe is a dream and when you physically die you awaken to your real and eternal life."

Is this my guardian angel here with me, speaking to me? My ghostly pilot? I want to see the figure in the bow more clearly but can't. Now I can't see it at all. The apparition has vanished, but the blissful light continues to envelop us. God is this light, this perfect bliss; a light like none seen on physical earth. I am this light of Paradise; so is Kathy and, potentially, every human being. This radiance *is* Paradise *here now*. This is why, detached from my body, I have never been more alive. *This is our real life;* normal consciousness is death.

Gradually I return to the mundane world and problems of *Fidelio* and become aware of Kathy watching me from the companionway. When she sees that I have returned to normal consciousness, she climbs into the cockpit, kneels beside me, and puts her arms around me, murmuring, "Oh, my dear, my dear." Her beautiful eyes, filled with tears, complete this moment of magic.

Then, according to Kathy, I sat down in my seat at the table and wrote down what I had seen while she was cooking breakfast. Only I have no recollection at all of doing this. Yet there are the entries in the logbook in my normal handwriting. "Automatic" writing? I have no explanation.

3:00 P.M.—All afternoon I have been scanning the horizon for a glimpse of Vieques; the closer we can get to it the better. But no sign of it yet. In fact, as we close the coast of Puerto Rico I have the impression that we are close to where we were yesterday at this time. A bearing confirms this impression. We have gained only two or three miles of easting—twenty-four hours of struggling for nothing! During the storm we drifted downwind for almost four hours, and coming back with the torn mainsail *Fidelio* obviously hasn't been sailing as close to the wind as she normally does.

Now I make plans to revise our itinerary. Instead of sailing from St. Croix to St. Thomas to Fajardo as planned, we will sail from Fajardo to St. Thomas to St. Croix.

Columbus departed from St. Croix on November 14, 1493, immediately encountered bad weather, and hove the fleet to. The next morning he saw numerous islands to the north; so many, in fact, that he was inspired to name the group after Saint Ursula and the 11,000 virgins of Cologne. Of course, there are nowhere near 11,000 Virgin Islands, just as we can safely assume that there were not 11,000 virgins among those adventurous maidens who sailed with Saint Ursula from Cologne to Rome. Maybe the true number was more like 11.

After examining the Virgins the fleet headed west and about twenty miles from St. Thomas came upon a verdant island, which Columbus named Gratiosa, which today is known as Vieques (or crab). From here Columbus could clearly see the impressive mountains of Puerto Rico. Doubtless, the summits were obscured by clouds as they were when we first sighted them.

Columbus's fleet then sailed along the south coast so, approaching from Vieques, they must have closed the land near or a few miles to the east of Tuna Point. In short, while we have missed his route along the Leewards, at least we will be retracing the route of his ships as they sailed downwind through Vieques Channel.

Columbus named the large island San Juan Bautista, but the name did not stick, due to the energetic activities of one of his shipmates. Ponce de Leon gazed at the rich coastal plains backed by towering mountains and resolved to return and conquer the island for himself. He made his wild dream come true thirteen years later; so much so that today just about everything on the island seems to bear his name.

He founded the city of San Juan with its magnificent harbor, which prompted the name San Juan de Puerto Rico, or Saint John of the Rich Harbor. Eventually, the entire island became known as Puerto Rico.

On his fourth and final voyage to the New World, Columbus first saw Martinique on June 15, 1502, after a fast passage of only twenty-one days from the Canaries. This gives some idea of the speed of sixteenth-century caravels when running downwind. After resting and re-filling his casks with fresh water, which in some places on this spectacular island cascades straight down the mountain sides and into the sea, Columbus proceeded directly to Santo Domingo. Presumably, he passed south of Islas de Aves; if so, *Fidelio* must have paralleled or crossed his track at some point.

But now, unlike Columbus we are headed east rather than west, which means the wind is right on the nose for anyone heading up the Vieques Channel. Moreover, as the sun sinks the wind picks up once again. The morning's calm couldn't last. Now about Force 6, an ideal wind for *Fidelio* to beat up the channel in, even though it would mean a lot of tacking. For *Fidelio,* yes; for me, no. I've had it. I want off, and so does Kathy. Easier said than done. If I'm ever going to make it to Fajardo I am now convinced that it won't be accomplished by sailing with a torn mainsail. So I drop the sails and fire up the Volvo. By nightfall we are opposite the entrance to the big naval base at Roosevelt Roads, just as a frigate glides out and passes to port. On the right a mile or so distant are the lights of the elusive Vieques Island.

Now a series of rain-filled squalls adds to our misery. An hour later we round the last headland and steer 351° as directed by the *Yachtman's Guide to Puerto Rico and the Virgin Islands.*

The channel is narrow, with reefs and low-lying is-lands on either side. I know that the correct seamanlike ac-tion would be to anchor for the night, but I am too tired to use good judgment. Another hour passes. I nod off, then jerk awake: breakers dead ahead! I put the helm hard over and we crunch and then go bump! bump! bump! over a coral head and are back in the channel. This life will be the end of me yet! Even Kathy, who is warming some cocoa, looks worried and exhausted.

About 11:30 P.M. she sees a buoy, and we run up to it. The number does not agree with the one shown on the chart at this position. I turn back to locate the last one behind us. After groping around another half hour, I steer 295° for the Conquistador Hotel, whose lights blazing out over Vieques Sound from a high hill have been visible for some time.

Another hour of searching back and forth, barely missing the ever-present reefs, and we finally locate the channel buoys leading into Fajardo harbor and the anchorage area at Isleta Marina.*

Finally we anchor, in pouring rain, at 2:00 A.M. after narrowly avoiding a collision with another yacht. We are so tired that we are punch-drunk, but still not too tired for a nightcap of the traditional sailor's drink—rum. We clink

---

* The next morning when we walk around the island we look with horror at the extensive array of reefs that menace the harbor entrance. How we came through safely in the dark is beyond me. A complicating factor was that the *Yachtman's Guide,* about which I can't say too many good things, showed a fine picture of Isleta Marina—a typical small coral island with one or two one-story buildings where the marina is housed. But as we approached the Conquistador Hotel (which couldn't be mistaken) where Isleta should be, there are two huge condominium towers. Where were we? What were they? Confusing at 1:00 A.M. after a difficult passage. The guide was only a year or two old, but those towers had been started right after it was published.

mugs while I make a final entry in the logbook: "Again, through the grace of God and my guardian angel, we made it safely to port, when we could have met with disaster, not once but many times."

After one drink we are so sleepy we barely make it to our forward double bunk where we curl up together. Kathy is asleep in seconds. I'm half asleep but still wonder, "Will *Fidelio* and I be able to persuade her to sail across the Pacific with us, or will she succeed in persuading me to return home with her?"